S. E. Thomas

Longing for Rest

A Novella

Longing for Rest
A Novella

Published by The Dramatic Pen Press, L.L.C.

Lolo, Montana

Copyright © 2014 S. E. Thomas

All rights reserved.
ISBN-10: 0692283803
ISBN-13: 978-0692283806

A great many thanks to my
friends, family, and fellow writers'
group members who encouraged me,
helped me edit, and pushed me
to better both my work and myself.

❧ Chapter One ❦

Crystal sunlight blinked through tree limbs, painting splotches of white across the blankets in the gray of the room. Amy stirred and breathed out heavily through her nose as if to chase the morning away. The speckled pattern of light played on her arm and half of her face each time the breeze blew. The window stood open. The gentle rustling of the leaves and that same annoying crow cawed loudly and repeatedly from a branch of her mountain ash tree. He was chasing away her dreams... strange, lost dreams. Part of her wanted to be rid of them and another part wanted to stay and straighten things out. But it was hopeless. She was nearly awake now.

One particularly brilliant bit of light glared down on her right eye. She opened her eyes. Only then did she realize that her left eye wouldn't open all the way. It struggled against crusty, dried tears from the night before. And suddenly she remembered.

A terrible weight landed on her chest. Without even looking she knew she was alone in the bed. Reality forced confirmation on her even as she tried again to return to the release of sleep. But there was no going back. She was fully awake now and she knew. Devon was gone. He was with Darla now.

Amy raised one weary hand to wipe the crust from her eye and found the flesh around her eye swollen and tender to the touch. As she rubbed, new tears flowed. Surprising. She thought she had used them all.

The blankets felt heavy. Her arms, too. The very air in the room crushed her. Breathing was a struggle. Amy rolled over onto her other side and realized the motion had been a terrible mistake. With it, her head began to throb with blinding intensity—her reward for giving into the racking sobs that had claimed her through much of the night.

How could this happen to me? How could Devon do this to me? What did I do to deserve this? Isn't he supposed to love me? Did he ever love me?

The questions repeated themselves in her mind as though put there by someone else. She fought them. She did not want to wrestle with them anymore. There were no answers. There might never be any answers.

Amy forced herself slowly onto one elbow against the protest of her throbbing head and weary body. She caught a quick glimpse of the clock before letting herself fall back onto the damp pillow. 6:57 AM. Thursday morning. In three minutes the alarm would go off, and it would be time to get the kids ready for school.

Why do I always wake up before the alarm? Why couldn't I sleep even a little longer on this horrible morning? Why do I have to wake up at all?

And then another horrible thought came to her.

The kids! They don't know yet! How am I going to tell them? What in the world can I possibly say to them? 'Kids, your father left us.' 'Kids, your father fell in love with someone else and moved out.' 'Kids, your father doesn't love me anymore and...'

A new wave of anger washed over her.

How dare he! How dare he leave me to explain all of this to his children! How dare he leave me at all!

The alarm blared. Amy wiped the fresh tears away and swung a heavy arm to turn off the buzzing. Michael and Cassandra still slept soundly in their beds, unmindful of how their world had toppled. Amy dreaded waking them, as she had never dreaded anything in her life. For fifteen minutes she stayed under the covers, trying to think of how she might tell them—what she would do, what she would say. But nothing sounded right. Nothing would ever be right.

Amy remembered with renewed dread that Devon had told her he would come by today on his lunch break. He wanted to collect some of his things. He'd be lucky if he didn't find his things sitting out on the curb when he drove up! But even that thought was not fully felt. Anger had not fully settled on her yet. It was all just so... unreal. No... maybe it was too real. And she didn't know how to understand it—how to believe it. But he would be there soon... too soon. How could she face him? And how could he face her? How could he come and look her in the face after what he had done?

I guess I'll find out soon enough.

Forcing herself from the bed, more of the scene from last night threatened to replay itself again in her memory. She pushed it back and stood, only to lean again on the side of the bed. She noticed a line of tight pain across her left side. She still wore her bra from yesterday. In fact, she had slept in her clothes—a blouse, now covered with wrinkles, and jean shorts. Amy stumbled against a new onslaught from her headache and made her way into the bathroom where she tried to avoid seeing the disheveled hair and the wan, puffy aftermath in the mirror. She downed four ibuprofen tablets. Amy then ran a washcloth under cold water and held it to her face. She pressed the coolness against her swollen eyes, hoping they would return to normal. How she wished everything would just return to normal.

Not now. Not this morning. I can't tell them this morning. There's no reason it has to be now. Let them go to school. I'll find some way to tell them later.

She took a deep breath and decided. Now she focused on hiding the effects the night, with its many sorrows, had left on her.

☾   ☾   ☾   ☾   ☾

"We will be touching down in Spokane, Washington in about ten minutes. Please return to your seats and fasten your seatbelts. Return seat backs and trays to their full, upright position. Please turn off and store all electronic devices. Thank you for flying Delta." The flight attendant's nasally voice clicked off the intercom followed by a 'dong' indicating that the seatbelt light again demanded obedience.

"Okay, kids," Monica said. "It's time to put your seatbelts back on."

Charity, sitting by the window to Monica's left had already latched her tray back into position and fumbled for her seatbelt. Monica glanced to the right at her son, Angel, and saw he hadn't even heard the announcement. He sat listening to Toby Mac through the earphones of his IPod while simultaneously reading a skateboarding magazine he had picked up during their layover in Salt Lake City.

"Angel…" No response. Monica pulled on one of the speaker wires until the speaker head popped out of his left ear. "Angel," she said too loudly, "it's time to turn off your music and put your seatbelt back on. We're almost there."

Angel obeyed by pushing the tiny button on his IPod but fought a scowl. "No me gusta cuando me llames eso," he mumbled just loud enough for her to hear.

"Please speak English. This is a good time to start practicing. None of my family speaks Spanish, you know, and I won't have you being rude to your relatives. And I'm going to call you by your name, not that silly nickname, so you might as well get used to it."

It had been a long trip, and Monica was in no mood to get involved in the same old argument with her fifteen-year-old son. She realized she had snapped at him and, while part of her felt guilty, the other part just felt tired and annoyed. His name was Angel—not an uncommon name for a Mexican boy—but he disliked it. He felt it wasn't masculine enough. Monica couldn't understand this since, to look at him, he was perhaps the most masculine of any in his circle of friends. Though tall, he had long since lost that spindly look. And his habit of weight-lifting since age eleven had added meat and muscle to his already broad shoulders. When standing next to him she already felt dwarfed. Monica was petite, slender and no more than five feet, three inches in heals. Her son looked like a man of twenty while most of his friends looked like they still needed babysitters.

Regardless, his friends had given him a nickname, which—for a reason unbeknownst to Monica—he seemed to prefer. They called him "Negro" or, sometimes, "Negrito", which means "Black One" or "Blacky". He had earned it due to his dark complexion, black eyes and jet-black hair. Though Monica was white, she had the darkest complexion of her family—dark brown, wavy hair, just past shoulder-length, and chocolate brown eyes. Whatever fair-skinned genes she had missed Angel completely. He was as dark, if not darker, than his Mexican father.

All the boys his age had nicknames—at least any boy who had friends—and these names generally centered on their less than admirable qualities. Only the lucky few received names that were due to a skill or an accomplishment. Most ended up fighting for -respect throughout adolescence. One of Angel's friends had been given the nickname "Cinturas" which means "Belts", because, though he wore belts every day, no one could ever see them under his large roll of belly fat.

Monica tried to remember Cinturas's real name but couldn't. She had started calling him "Cinturas", too, she realized. But Cinturas didn't seem to mind. In fact, none of the boys seemed to mind their nicknames, preferring instead to wear them like hard-earned badges of honor. She supposed it was a way to feel accepted by the group—like they had good enough friends to be mercilessly teased, or some backwards philosophy like that. Oh, well. She didn't mind when they called her son "Negro" but she certainly wasn't going to call him that. Let alone around her family! She could just hear it now— Louisa saying in her gringa, militant voice, "Negro! Who is Negro? Why in the world would you call your son that?"

Louisa. Monica sighed. *Will Louisa be there yet?*

Louisa had married Monica's brother, Kevin. Monica often wondered how those two had managed to stay married all these years. Now she wondered if what she had heard from her mother the last time they had talked was true. Were they really doing better, or had they just put on a happy face to please Mom? She would soon find out.

Lord, please help me deal with Louisa and watch my mouth, she prayed. *And maybe You can help her watch her mouth, too,* she added.

Kevin and Louisa were probably already there, she realized. In fact, they might even be waiting with Daniel in the baggage claim area in Spokane.

Daniel was Monica's oldest brother. He lived in Moscow, Idaho, where her mother also lived. He had told her he would pick up her and her kids, and that the drive to Moscow would take about an hour and a half. It would be nice to see Daniel again. She had missed him.

Kevin, Louisa, and their youngest son were supposed to be driving up from Texas. Monica hadn't heard if their oldest was coming. He attended grad school in Florida.

He was smart to get away from them, she thought and then regretted it.

But the truth remained that their oldest, Clark, seemed to be doing better than their youngest, Kenneth, who, at 21 years of age, still lived with them and had no ambition nor sense of direction at all.

Maybe things have changed, she told herself. *It's been three years since I've been home. Too long. I should've come sooner. I just didn't think I'd have to say goodbye to Mom so soon.*

Monica tried to silence that thought. She didn't want to think of her once vibrant and energetic mother lying in a hospital bed with tubes coming out of her. She didn't want to face losing her mother while her husband was still stuck in Tijuana trying to get his visa renewed. It had all happened so suddenly. She hadn't been ready for that early morning phone call or for Daniel's voice on the other end telling her their mother's kidneys had failed, and that she was in critical condition in the ICU.

Monica took a deep breath and steadied herself. She couldn't cry again—not now. They were almost there. What would the flight attendants think? And Angel was embarrassed enough by her already. She looked past her daughter out the window and watched the ground getting closer and closer, faster and faster. They heard the roar of the engines and both felt and heard the bump and then a bigger bump as they touched down.

Charity yawned and Monica found herself imitating her daughter, waiting for that satisfying feel of her ears popping and sounds becoming clearer. They still moved quickly along the ground, but she could feel the gentle tug of the plane slowing.

Charity stopped looking out the window long enough to return the book she had been holding to the backpack under the seat in front of her. Monica glanced at Angel as Charity zipped it closed. He looked back at her and must have read the worry in her face. He smiled. An encouraging smile. Monica had often thought her son to be short on smiles. She felt particularly grateful for this one. He had forgiven her for snapping at him, and she knew that even though her husband couldn't be there yet, Angel would be a support to her.

Such a nice name, Angel... I can't understand why he doesn't like it. It just suits him somehow.

€   €   €   €   €

How could he bring her *here?* Amy stood in her kitchen watching as Devon pulled up. He actually had Darla in the car with him, and they seemed to be having an animated discussion, hands flopping about, mouths agape. Devon opened his door and got out as Darla turned away from him with a look of annoyance. She rolled down her window and found a magazine.

Suddenly, the anger that had eluded Amy yesterday came upon her with a force that robbed her of her sanity.

How dare this woman come between my husband and me? How dare she step into my life and rob me this way? I hate her!

Amy experienced an overwhelming desire to run outside, reach through Darla's window, grab her by the hair and start banging her head on the windowsill of the car. She may have done it, too, if Devon hadn't opened the front door just then. Her attention shifted for a moment. There he was. Devon stood before her, eyes cast to the side and downwards, not looking at her.

A part of Amy rebelled against the way he had just walked into the house—claiming ownership of a space they had shared—a space he had forfeited. He said nothing. He kept his eyes down and seemed to be waiting for her to say something—perhaps to yell at him or even throw something.

Amy looked at his familiar face, light brown hair, dimpled chin. But she saw only a stranger.

Who is this man? Do I know him at all?

Devon cleared his throat and shifted from one foot to the other.

"Well," he said, "I came to get my things."

Amy found she could say nothing. All that had been swirling through her mind and tormenting her through the night—the many angry accusations, the questions full of hurt, the pleadings for him to come back. None of them seemed appropriate somehow. They all demanded an intimacy that no longer existed. The only thing that mattered right now was that he seemed intent on continuing with his plan to leave her, to move in with Darla, and to do his best to forget the fifteen years he had spent married to her.

Devon must have decided she had nothing to say to him. He turned abruptly on his heal and headed to their bedroom—no, her bedroom. Amy heard him opening drawers and then realized she had been holding her breath. She released it and it came out in a tattered, ragged sob. She quickly covered her mouth with her hand, fervently hoping he hadn't heard. She didn't want him to see how deeply he had wounded her. But she couldn't get hold of herself. A second sob followed the first. Then another and another—each more devastating to her composure than the last. Amy realized with unexpected rationality that she was becoming hysterical. She grabbed a chair and sat down heavily at the kitchen table.

Stop it! Stop it! Get a hold of yourself!

She put a hand on her chest and pressed, focusing all her strength and willpower on getting herself under control.

More rustling noises came from the bedroom. She realized they had stopped for a moment but now the sounds of packing resumed. He must have heard. He must have. She covered her mouth again, now only whimpering through heavy, sob-like breaths. She fought for control.

I'm okay. I'm okay. I'm okay.

Then Amy made the mistake of glancing out the window. When in the kitchen, she often enjoyed a glance upon her front garden that bloomed all year round and the quaint stone path that meandered through bright green grass. Seeing these things had always given her a sense of pride to live in such a well-kept home. Now she only saw Devon's car parked in front with Darla sitting in the passenger seat—in Amy's seat—looking bored.

The rage returned in an instant. Amy stopped crying. She stood up and a wrath-filled cry of fury wrenched from her. She sounded like a lioness on the hunt but this time gave not a thought to the fact that Devon would have heard her. Somehow her hand found a rolling pin that had been left lying on the counter. With weapon in hand Amy tore from the kitchen, out of the house, and toward the car.

That tramp thinks this is boring? Just some little inconvenience in her day? Does she think this is some kind of a game?

By the time these thoughts had processed, Amy was already at the car.

"What are you doing?" Darla screamed, terror distorting her pretty face.

"You're going to find out!" was all Amy could get out before sending the rolling pin smashing into the windshield of the passenger side. "You think you can steal my husband?" Another splintering crash and a scream of panic from Darla. "You think you can come to my home and destroy my family?" Another crash. This time the rolling pin went all the way through, and shards of glass sprayed across Darla's face. A few of them landed in her open, screaming mouth. "You think you're playing some kind of a game?"

Amy raised the rolling pin to smash more of the glass but found that it caught in mid-air behind her. Before she knew what was happening, Devon's strong arms wrapped around her, restraining her. His touch made her stomach turn and her heart feel like it might explode into flames.

She struggled and kicked and screamed, "Let me go! Let me go!"

"Stop it! Stop it!" he yelled as he wrenched the weapon from her with his free one and threw it to the ground.

"Let me go! Don't touch me!"

Devon released her, and she slumped to the ground. Sobs overtook her again, and she sat in a heap and buried her face in her hands.

What's happened? How have I been reduced to this? What has become of me?

Darla had stopped screaming, and Amy thought she heard the sound of her whimpering, spitting—glass, probably—and brushing off her clothes at the same time. Devon stood over Amy for a moment, saying nothing.

He pities me, she thought, disgusted with herself but still unable to manage her sobbing. *He pities me. I'm pitiable. I lost my husband and now I've lost my dignity. I have nothing left.*

"Have you gone mad?" Devon finally said in an angry whisper. "What are the neighbors going to think? I mean, look what you did to the car!"

He's crazier than I am, Amy thought with dismay, but didn't look up.

"Get me out of here!" Darla finally got enough glass out of her mouth to screech at him. "Why are you just standing there? Your wife just tried to kill me!"

Devon glanced at her and answered in an annoyed voice, "She did not!"

Amy found his defense strange.

"Get your stuff and let's go!" Darla ordered.

Devon seemed hesitant. "Look," he said finally to Amy. "I'm going to get my things now. And for heaven's sake, don't do anything crazy!" He picked up the rolling pin before heading back to the house. He went quickly, shooting a nervous glance at her before disappearing inside.

A few seconds ticked by. Darla fidgeted in her seat. "Look," she said. "I'm sorry this is so... so... hard on you right now."

Amy ignored her, still crying, face in her hands, hiding from the world.

"It just wasn't working out between you two," Darla foolishly continued. "You'll both be better off in the long run. He just needed to make a change, that's all... he needed—"

"Shut up!" Amy said, pronouncing each word in measured staccato. She stood. Somehow her composure—or some of it—returned. She approached the window, and Darla scooted as far away as the seatbelt allowed. "Don't think you can tell me anything about my husband! I've known him for eighteen years! I've been married to him for fifteen of those, and in that time I've gotten to know him a little better than you do! So, spare me the explanations! Spare me the advice! Spare me the—"

"Hey! What are you doing?" Devon's worried voice came from the porch. He came swiftly to them, a suitcase in each hand. "What are you doing?" he repeated. "Get away from the car, Amy."

"It's my car," Amy replied with deathlike calmness.

Darla stared at her with a mixture of hatred and fear. Devon stepped around Amy and opened the back door. He threw the suitcases onto the back seat and slammed the door shut again.

"Have you told the kids yet?" he asked as he opened the driver's side door.

"I thought you should tell them," Amy lied. She wouldn't dream of allowing him to have a chance to lie to them, justify himself to them, or manipulate them—but she wanted him to squirm, to realize how difficult a position he had placed their family in.

He rewarded her with a look of anger and consternation. He seemed unsure of how to respond. "Fine!" he yelled. He got in and slammed the door. His anger intensified when he found prickly shards of glass under his buttocks. He started from the discomfort and then shifted to brush them away. He started the engine but, before driving away said, "I'll call them tonight."

❧ Chapter Two ⚜

"Monica," the familiar voice of her brother broke through the crowd of people in the baggage claim area.

"Daniel!" Monica rushed to him and wrapped him in a warm embrace. He stood much taller and broader than she, and his long, strong arms seemed to cover every inch of her back. It felt good.

"Hey, kids!" He released her to hug his niece and nephew. "My goodness! You two are practically grown!"

Though Daniel's voice contained his familiar warmth, Monica could see the fatigue and worry written in the lines on his brow, the slight droop of his shoulders, and the lightless gaze in his eyes. She also noticed he had put on at least fifteen pounds since the last time she saw him, and his hair, once a deep brown, now grayed at the temples.

After a brief greeting, Angel spotted one of their bags going around on the carousel and went to retrieve it.

"Wow! He's gotten big!" Daniel commented as Angel walked away.

"I know. I brought him along to carry the bags," Monica joked.

"He looks like he could carry them all."

"Not the way Charity packs."

"Hey!" Charity interjected. "I only brought the essentials."

"Oh? Your bubble-gum wrapper collection is an essential?" her mother jibed.

"I wanted to show Grandma."

Monica's smile faded. She suddenly felt very tired. Tired from the journey, yes, but more still from worry. And from the worry lines on Daniel's face, she knew it wouldn't get any better right away.

"Stay here. I'll help Angel," Daniel said and approached the youth as he attempted to rescue three bags at once from escaping through the hatch.

A few moments later, he opened the hatchback and helped Angel load the baggage. Then he climbed into the driver's seat next to Monica and said, "Everybody in?" The sound of Angel's door closing confirmed it, and Daniel started the engine and pulled slowly from the loading zone.

As they left the terminal in Daniel's green GMC Jimmy, he asked his sister, "So, how was the trip?"

"It was alright, I guess. We got all our luggage back."

"What time did you leave this morning?"

"The house or San Diego?"

"Both."

"Well, we woke up at three A.M. and left the house by 3:30. Then we had to drive from Tijuana to the San Diego airport. It's not far, but you have to give yourself plenty of time—just in case the border patrol decides you look like a drug smuggler. Thankfully, we passed this time. Our plane left San Diego at 6:15, and then we had about a two-hour layover in Salt Lake."

"Are you hungry?" he asked. It was already half past noon, and his stomach had just let out a loud growl. "There's not much between here and Moscow, but I can stop at that big 76 station if you want. They've got those pre-made deli sandwiches and stuff like that."

"No, we're good. We grabbed an early lunch in Salt Lake. The earlier you wake up, the earlier you get hungry."

"I'll just stop and grab myself something, then, if that's all right."

"Sure."

They lapsed into a few moments of silence. Monica knew what she wanted to ask, but was afraid to ask it. As it turned out, she didn't have to.

"Mom's not doing well," he began, and she could tell he was trying to ease into the bad news. "She's in a coma, Monica."

Monica hadn't prepared for this. She knew it was bad. She thought her mother might even have passed away sometime while they were still in the air; but this?

"What—what do you mean?" she stammered. "How did this happen?"

"She was pretty bad when they brought her in. Apparently, her blood was already too polluted—too much potassium—or something like that. You'll have to let the doctor explain it to you, but that's what happens when the kidneys fail. She started feeling real sick a couple of days before. She thought she had the flu or something."

"Yes, you told me most of this on the phone last night," Monica tried to keep the impatience from her voice, but couldn't tell if she managed.

"Right, well, the doctors diagnosed her with a severe case of uremia when she came in. Uremia is when the levels of toxins in the blood are too high. That was at about midnight last night. I called you shortly after that. They put her on dialysis, but at about five-thirty this morning she slipped into a coma."

"But what about the dialysis? Didn't it work?"

"I asked about that, too. The doctor said when the blood toxins are that high it takes several sessions before the blood is sufficiently cleaned. Each session takes about three hours. She wasn't even finished with her second session when she lost consciousness."

"But can they wake her? What are they going to do?"

Daniel sighed and watched the road. They neared the 76 on the right. He pulled in and parked before answering.

"I think we have to prepare ourselves for the worst, Monica. Dr. Riley talked with me at some length, and, from what he said, I just don't think there's much hope."

"I'd like to speak to this Dr. Riley myself!"

Daniel reached over and put his large, warm hand over hers and squeezed it. At his touch, hot tears dribbled from her eyes and slid down her cheeks.

"Getting angry with the doctor is not going to help," he said softly. "I think this guy knows what he's doing. He's a good doctor. I've heard this from others, too, and he's taken a lot of time to help me understand what's going on with her. He'll do the same for you. But he can't work miracles, Monica. He said Mom most likely has already sustained some serious heart damage and other—"

"He can't work miracles, but God can!" Monica interrupted defiantly, angrily.

Daniel looked at her steadily. He nodded. "Yes. You're right. God can. We should keep praying."

When she said nothing else, he gave her hand one last squeeze and got out of the car. She watched him walk across the narrow parking lot and enter the 76.

"Mom?" a timid voice came from the back.

"Yes, Charity?"

"Is Grandma going to die?"

A heavy sigh escaped Monica and she fought for control. More tears slid unbidden down her cheeks. "I don't know, honey. I think we need to pray."

☾   ☾   ☾   ☾   ☾

"Turn left!"

Kevin bit back his annoyance with his wife and made the swift left turn, clipping the curb as he went.

"Hey!" Kenneth's complaint at the jolt sounded from the back seat. "Someone's trying to read back here!"

"I thought you knew this town," Louisa said.

"You can go the other way, too," Kevin responded through tightened jaws with a quick glance her way.

Suddenly Louisa screamed, "Look out!"

Kevin looked back to the road just in time to see a car coming straight toward them in their lane. He slammed on the brakes and felt his son's body slam into the back of his seat.

"Oh, no!" Louisa cried in fright. "Ahhhh!" She braced herself against the dash with both hands and lifted her right knee into a defensive position.

The other driver saw him at the last second and swerved back into his own lane, narrowly avoiding a head-on collision.

"Is everybody all right? Kenneth?" Kevin demanded, focusing his concern on the back seat.

"I'm all right," Kenneth's voice sounded muffled and too low. Kevin wrenched against his seatbelt to turn and look into the back. He saw Kenneth crawl from the floor of the car and return to his seat. "I'd like to make it to my

22nd birthday, if you don't mind! Ow!" Kenneth gripped his right wrist with his left hand and rubbed.

"Are you hurt, Honey?" Louisa asked in alarm.

"I think it's just a sprain," he said with a grimace and let out a heavy breath.

Kevin sighed in an attempt to get his heart beating normally again. He started forward and saw in the rearview mirror a large truck directly behind him. He realized, with a new wave of anxiety mixed with relief, the miracle that they hadn't been rear-ended.

"What in the world was that guy thinking?" Louisa's anger found a new outlet. "What a maniac! Did you see him?"

"Of course he saw him, Mom. He stopped, didn't he?" Kenneth said as he searched around the floor for his book.

"For heaven's sake, put your seatbelt on!" Louisa ordered. "I can't believe they let some people on the road!"

"Hey, did you see his windshield? It was all smashed in—like they'd already been in an accident today," Kenneth said.

"I think he was drunk!" Louisa said, still flustered.

"No," Kevin interjected as he made a right turn. "They were arguing. The couple in the car—I think they were arguing."

☾   ☾   ☾   ☾   ☾

"AGH!" Darla's scream, like that of a drowning cat, sent Devon's attention back to his driving. At first horrified to see another car in his lane, in an instant he realized he was the one who had veered to the wrong side of the road. He swerved to the right, missing the oncoming car but overcorrected and almost hit a parked car on the other side. Darla screamed again, but somehow Devon managed to right the vehicle.

"What are you doing?" Darla demanded hotly.

"If you hadn't been badgering me, that wouldn't have happened!"

"Don't blame me! You're the one with the death wish here! Oh, my heart!" She grasped at her full, heaving chest. "You almost gave me a heart attack! You almost got us killed!"

Devon also struggled to get his emotions under control but said, "We wouldn't have been killed! Banged up pretty good maybe, but we weren't going fast enough to be killed."

"This is too much! Twice in one day! I've nearly been killed twice in one day! I can't believe it!"

"Don't get hysterical! You have not!"

Darla turned to him, eyes blazing. "First, your wife tries to bludgeon me to death with a rolling pin, and then you try to have a head-on collision with another car!"

"She didn't try to kill you! Don't start that again!"

Darla turned her eyes to the street in front of her. "Pay attention to the road!" she cried.

Devon noticed that once again his eyes had strayed from the street ahead. Driving with Darla in the car proved dangerous. Normally, her passionate nature drew him, excited him, made him want to be near her—possess her. This energy had first caused him to notice her, had tempted him and, eventually, enticed him into a completely new existence. At the moment, though, he found her emotional heights highly irritating. Funny he hadn't noticed this before.

Darla lived 'over the top.' Her voice could often be heard across the office floor in the real estate building where they both worked. She talked loudly and laughed even louder. She made people feel liked and special. Also incredibly beautiful, it was no wonder her sales always surpassed his and every other agent's in town. One smile from those perfect lips and people were sold.

From the first day she joined his team, Devon fought an attraction to her. He knew for a fact that at least two of his male co-workers also harbored feelings for her—one of them nearly twice her age and married, he thought with disgust. But, did he really have the right to blame them? Darla's slender but full-figured frame, red hair, and luxurious, emerald green eyes begged men to notice. And, despite the rumor in the office that she'd had some work done, Devon couldn't tell the difference. Nor did he care. She looked like a girl from a magazine. Even so, he might still have remained faithful to his wife and just been satisfied with watching her from afar. But Darla had a way of knowing. She had a sixth sense that detected attraction in men. And she spotted his long before he did.

It was all very innocent at first. Darla even turned up at church once. When she saw him there, she kept coming. Amy had met Darla there, so Devon let her believe he, too, only ever saw Darla at church. He didn't know why he felt the need to keep this part of his working life to himself. He figured later he could just say his association with her had never come up. In a way, since Darla attended church now, he felt safer with her—telling himself she was just another Christian sister. But at work, Devon and Darla lingered at the coffee maker, teased one another about sales, and gossiped about clients.

At business lunches and meetings he found himself jockeying for a seat next to her or, better still, across from her. He liked to watch her mouth as she talked. Before long, he began to focus on other parts of her anatomy as well, appreciating Darla's fearlessness at wearing low-cut V-neck tops, short skirts, and stiletto pumps. Often, she dropped by his desk to ask him a question about a legal matter or a listing. She had a habit of standing opposite him and leaning forward across his desk, giving him a full view of her more than ample cleavage. It took all his mental powers to answer even her simplest questions. Soon, Darla became a regular fixture in his fantasies.

Within three months they exchanged group business lunches for private ones. It was still innocent, he told himself. What's lunch with a business colleague? Nothing. In fact, it would be sexist to treat her differently than any other member of the team.

Soon, however, private lunches became private dinners. He told Amy business called him away and, during the meal, even made sure to throw in a few comments about the job to feel he wasn't lying. Before long, though, they no longer discussed work. She began to confide in him about past relationships, her father's inattention, her feelings of inadequacy. And, despite her ability to capture a crowd with her voice, he found her to be a good listener, too. And so he talked. He started talking about seemingly inconsequential matters—fond childhood memories, his kids' activities, his ambitions. Then, he started sharing deeper things—how he felt distant from his wife, his inability to be himself at home, how Amy had let herself go.

Private dinners out became private dinners in. And just as he began to recognize the slippery slope, he found himself at the bottom of it. Darla stood before him dressed in something she had called 'more comfortable,' though comfort was definitely not what the designers had in mind when creating this tiny, black, lace number that now clung loosely to Darla's perfect, nearly bare frame. Wow! Did she look amazing! And she was right there... stunning... and available.

Now, though, sitting in a smashed up car beside her, with his emotions heightened in a completely opposite vein, he realized that sometimes the most important decisions are the ones you don't seem to make at all. At the time it seemed so natural. And later, when the guilt hit him like a line drive to the gut, he simply used it to fuel further interactions with her. After all, he'd already become intimate with her. Going back to how it was before was no longer an option. Might as well go forward and pursue what he really wanted.

Devon swallowed hard to recover his composure and refocused on his driving.

"It's hard to see the road with the windshield all smashed," he muttered lamely, but was instantly sorry he'd said it. His excuse only supplied Darla with more ammunition.

"And whose fault is that? You shouldn't have left that woman alone!"

Perhaps I shouldn't have left her at all, Devon thought in his annoyance. But when he said nothing, Darla calmed a shade.

"At least, now we know what she's capable of," she said. "Maybe she'll learn her lesson when you file a police report against her."

"I'm not going to file a police report."

"Why not? She attacked me, and look what she did to the car!"

"What good would it do, Darla? She didn't actually touch you, did she? And it's not illegal to smash your own car. They wouldn't do anything about it."

"Humph!" Darla said in irritation. "Serve and protect! Yeah, right!" But mercifully, she lapsed into an angry silence.

☾   ☾   ☾   ☾   ☾

"Dr. Riley? This is my sister, Monica."

"Oh, hello." Dr. Riley turned from the chart he examined and held out a hand.

Monica extended hers and found his handshake warm and gentle, like his eyes. It would be hard to stay angry with this man, she realized. He put one arm on her back in a comforting gesture and said, "I'm sorry about your mother, Ma'am. I wish we could have met under better circumstances but I want you to know she's getting the best care possible and that I'd be happy to answer any questions you have."

"Thank you, Dr. Riley. I would really appreciate that. I do have some questions."

"Sure." He stepped back from her. "Come this way." He led Monica and Daniel into a private room—probably used for consultation purposes—and showed them each to a chair. Angel and Charity stayed in the waiting room. Janna and Kimberly, Daniel's two youngest daughters, had come down from their grandmother's room to meet them, and they now sat together getting reacquainted.

Dr. Riley perched himself on the edge of a desk. "Now, then, I suppose you've heard some of it from your brother, but I can start from the beginning, if you like."

Monica just nodded. So many questions swam through her mind that she didn't know what to ask first.

"Well, Mrs. Bennett—I mean, your mother—was brought in just after midnight last night. She was conscious then, but barely. I understand she had called you, Mr. Bennett. Is that right?"

"Yes," Daniel answered. "She called me complaining that she didn't feel well, so I went over to see her. I knew, if she had taken the time to call me, it was serious."

Monica nodded in knowing agreement. Her mother had never been one to complain about "piddly matters", as she called them. If she had felt ill enough to call Daniel in the middle of the night, it would be important.

"When we admitted her," Dr. Riley continued, "she complained of nausea, vomiting, extreme fatigue, headache, shortness of breath, and dimness of vision—all symptoms of kidney failure but also symptoms of a myriad of other problems. So, I ran some blood and urine tests and made a diagnosis...." He paused. "She is suffering from acute kidney failure. We gave her a diuretic and calcium—to help clean out the buildup of potassium in her blood and protect the heart—and we put her on dialysis right away."

"Daniel said something about heart damage." Monica meant it as a question.

Dr. Riley's face remained gentle, but his eyes grew serious. "I'm afraid so. There's reason to believe that the impure blood has already damaged your mother's heart. Her heart is also surrounded by a buildup of fluid that is causing it to have difficulty pumping." He moved his hands in a circular motion over his chest as he spoke.

"What do you do for that?"

"Well, your mother slipped into a coma, as I'm sure your brother told you."

Monica nodded.

"I don't think we can risk surgery at this time to drain the excess fluids. She is in a very precarious place, and it's doubtful she would survive the surgery. So, I'd like to give the dialysis a chance to return her blood chemistry to normal before we do anything more drastic."

Monica nodded again and glanced at Daniel. He still watched Dr. Riley, waiting for more. Dr. Riley complied, sensing the lull.

"I should tell you, Monica, that even with the dialysis, your mother may not survive."

Monica swallowed hard. She didn't want to hear this.

"The coma worries me greatly," he continued. "It's a sign that the blood is polluted enough to have interfered with normal brain function. And, as I'm sure you know, that can be very serious."

Monica nodded but couldn't face him anymore. New tears burned her eyes, and as she looked down, they splashed onto her folded hands. Daniel put a hand on her shoulder.

"I'm sorry," Dr. Riley said. "I know this is very difficult. But it's important that you know the truth. She could pass at any moment."

"I want to see her," Monica managed.

"Of course." Dr. Riley led them back into the waiting room where they met the others. "We can all go in and see her now."

The small entourage took the elevator to the third floor where Dr. Riley escorted them past the thick ICU doors into a sterile-smelling hospital room. The beep-beep of the heart monitor greeted them as they entered, as did the solemn smile of a nurse, who listened to Mrs. Bennett's lungs with a stethoscope. The brightness of the room struck Monica as odd, but what did she expect? Certainly, they wouldn't keep the room dark at all times for someone in a coma—as if they wanted her to keep sleeping.

Celia, Daniel's wife, and Halley, his oldest daughter, stood as they entered. Celia wore dark glasses and gripped a cane at her side. The reality of Celia's blindness struck Monica. She had heard, of course, about her sister-in-law's battle with glaucoma and how her sight had finally failed her. She had even prayed and fasted with her church in Tijuana for Celia when the doctors had given up hope. But to see her now, completely blind, she realized she had forgotten. She had forgotten to prepare herself for it in the wake of her worry for her mother.

"Celia," she said as she walked over to join her at her mother's bedside.

"Monica?" Celia held out her hands into the darkness before her, and Monica took them and pulled her close. As she embraced her sister-in-law, she glanced down at her mother. It was strange to see her mother's likeness on the face of that pale, deathlike figure lying on the bed. Oxygen tubes filled her nostrils and several more tubes draped about the bed, running out of her—or going into her. One carried a clear liquid, another carried blood, and there were more.

"Yes, it's me. How are you?"

"I'm fine," Celia said and Monica believed her.

They parted and Monica hugged Halley, Daniel and Celia's light-haired 21-year-old daughter. "Did you come from school to be here?"

"Yes, but I go to the University of Idaho, so I'm right here in town. I already got permission from my professors to make up my work later. They understand."

Monica hugged her again, "You're a good girl, Halley."

Then Monica turned to her mother. Halley found Monica a chair and brought it over to the side of the bed. She sat and Charity stood next to her. Charity began crying. Angel stood at the foot of the bed saying nothing and looking awkward and solemn.

Monica gently lifted her mother's right hand and held it in hers. It didn't feel like her mother's hand. It looked pale and puffy from the swelling—as did her whole arm, in fact—and the skin flaked dry and cracked from dryness. But what disturbed Monica most was that her mother's hand didn't react at all to her touch.

❧ Chapter Three ❧

Amy started at the sudden sound of ringing. But, recognizing the noise of the phone, she dropped an arm over her eyes and refused to move from the couch. The answering machine picked up. Devon's voice spoke clearly into the room, "You have reached the home of Devon, Amy, Michael and Cassandra. We're not in. You know what to do." Beep!

I'm going to have to change that recording.

"Amy? This is Idalee! I'm back from my vacation, and I want to tell you all about it! Call me!" Click. Beep!

I don't care about your vacation.

Idalee had been Amy's best friend for the better part of a decade. Funny, energetic, bubbly—not at all the kind of person Amy wanted to talk to right now. In fact, she despised the idea of talking to anyone. She just wished she could sleep and make everything disappear. But it was three o'clock. Michael and Cassandra, at this moment, were hearing the last bells of their school day. They were heading to their lockers, bumping into friends in the hallways, meeting one another in the parking lot, heading home. Amy only had about fifteen minutes before they walked in the door, maybe twenty, if they lingered. Not enough time for her to think of something to say—some way of telling them about their father.

Amy hadn't moved from the couch since Devon and Darla drove off together in her smashed car.

What was I thinking? How could I have lost it like that? That's not like me.

And she had seen the surprise—even disbelief—in Devon's eyes. He looked at her as though he'd never really seen her before. Perhaps he hadn't.

Amy took a deep breath and forced herself from the cushions. She trudged to her room to run a comb through her hair. The washcloth on her sink still felt damp, but she again ran it under fresh, cold water and held it to her face for a long moment. She tried not to think about Devon—only about Michael and Cassandra. They needed her to be strong. They needed her to be collected and reasonable—to have answers. But she didn't feel strong, she didn't feel collected or reasonable, and she certainly didn't have any answers.

The front door opened with a bang, and the sound mingled with Cassandra's voice. Amy couldn't make out the words until she heard, "Mom! We're home!"

Amy dropped the washcloth and dried her face. "I'm in my bathroom! Come and sit on my bed!"

Was the bedroom a good choice for this conversation? She didn't know. No good place existed. It just had to be done. She walked out of the bathroom at the same time her kids stepped through her bedroom door.

"You wanted to talk to us?" Cassandra asked.

"Did we do something wrong?" Michael wanted to know.

"No, no. Sit here on the bed with me."

"What's going on?" Cassandra asked as she claimed Devon's pillow as a seat.

Michael sat at the foot of the bed, studying her with concern in his eyes. Michael, the oldest at fourteen and two years older than his sister, was still far too young for this. Amy looked at him and sighed. She knew what she would tell him would make him feel like the man of the house. And he wasn't ready.

"It's about your father," Amy began and immediately realized those had not been the right words.

"What happened?" Cassandra asked, eyes wide with alarm. "Is he okay? Is he hurt? Is he—" Her frightened eyes finished for her.

"He's fine. He's fine." Amy said. *Perhaps this would be easier if he was dead.* "He isn't hurt. But things have changed for us and you need to know about it." Amy picked up her own pillow and squeezed it into her lap, letting her fingers massage the full corners as she gathered her thoughts.

"Where is he, Mom?" Michael asked.

"He won't be coming home for a while." She paused, and they waited for her to explain. "Do you remember how he didn't come home last night before you went to bed?"

They nodded. It happened a lot recently.

"Well, he did come home later. It was very late, and you were both already asleep. That's when he told me he's moving out."

Michael and Cassandra just looked at her in wide-eyed shock. Michael seemed to be trying to formulate an appropriate response but couldn't.

"I'm sorry. I'm so sorry this is happening." Again, the wrong words. Tears started from her eyes and were soon matched by some from Cassandra's. Michael's face deepened to pink. "Your father loves you very much, but he needs to live somewhere else for a while. He is going through a confusing time right now."

"What do you mean? What happened?" Michael's voice was hard, edgy, combative.

Amy paused. Should she tell them about Darla? Would they even understand? What about when they saw their father with Darla? If she didn't tell them now, how would she explain it later? And what if all of this blew over and Devon came back? She closed her eyes. She remembered Devon's eyes—full of determination on the night he told her he was leaving. He had been sure, confident, and had already made his plans. This would not just blow over.

"Your father has met someone else," she said as simply as she could. "He decided he would rather be with her than with me… and so he went away to see if he could make that work. I want you to know that you did nothing, nothing to make this happen. This isn't your fault. This is between your father and me. It has nothing to do with you." But those weren't exactly the right words either. It had everything to do with them. They would have to live with this abandonment for the rest of their lives.

"Does this mean you're going to get a divorce?" Cassandra asked through a voice stained with tears.

"I don't know…. Probably."

Cassandra hung her head and cried. Her sobs sounded hopeless and lost. Michael cried too, but his tears were angry, and his face finally achieved a deep red. He stood and clenched his fists. "How could he do this? Why couldn't you make him stay?" Michael fled the room, pounding his hurt into the carpet as he went.

"Michael!" Cassandra called after him. "Don't say that! It's not her fault! Michael!"

"It's alright, Cassandra, let him go. He's angry and hurt right now."

What Michael said hurt, but Amy had asked herself the same thing. Why couldn't she make him stay? What had she done to drive him away?

Cassandra scooted over to her mother and clung to her. "Is Daddy coming back?"

"He said he would call you later today. You can ask him."

☾   ☾   ☾   ☾   ☾

"Mrs. Bennett is in Room 310 on the third floor," an attractive female receptionist with a pixie cut and big, blue eyes answered Kevin. "You can go right up." She smiled. "The elevator is down the hall and to the right."

"Thank you," he responded and then turned to Louisa and Kenneth. "Shall we?"

They waited for the elevator to return to the ground floor.

"I wonder who's here already," Louisa said, tackling her thick, auburn hair with quick, nervous pats.

"Daniel said he was going to pick up Monica and her family at the airport," Kevin answered her. "They're probably here and Daniel's family, too, I would guess."

"Do you think Celia is here?"

"Why wouldn't she be?"

The elevator door opened and they entered. Kevin pushed the button marked 3.

"Oh, I don't know."

"She's blind, Mom, not crippled," Kenneth said with a roll of his eyes.

"I know! I know! It's just that I haven't seen her since she completely lost her sight…. I'm not sure what to say to her."

"Well, if you're quiet enough, she won't even know you're there," Kenneth said.

"Enough!" Kevin reprimanded his son. "Good grief, could you try to behave for just a few minutes, please? Is that too much to ask?"

"Sorry, Dad."

"Just treat her like you always have," Kevin returned his attention to Louisa with a deep breath. "You haven't seen her in several months. She'd probably like a hug."

"You're right," Louisa answered. "I don't know what I was thinking." Then she turned on her son, "And Kenneth, you need to watch your mouth!"

"Yes, Mom. I'll be a perfect little angel."

"Oh!" Louisa said. "Do you think Angel's here? He's such a handsome little boy."

The elevator stopped and dinged. The doors began to open.

"We'll soon find out," Kevin responded. "And I doubt he's little anymore."

Louisa's high heels clacked on the polished tile and echoed from the smooth, white walls as they walked down the corridor towards the ICU. Two metal doors barred the entrance. Kevin tried it and found them locked. Through the long, thin windows they could see nurses chatting to one another across a paper-piled counter. One of them noticed Kevin and made a jabbing motion, pointing him to his left.

He glanced over and at the same time Louisa said, "I think we're supposed to announce ourselves here."

A small gray box that looked like an intercom terminal had been screwed to the wall. It bore one small, round button directly in its center. Louisa pushed it.

"We're here to visit Mrs. Bennett," she spoke into the small grill in elevated staccato as she held down the button. Silence.

Then a static-mingled voice answered, "Who are you here to see?"

"I don't think you have to hold down the button," Kevin said. "Just talk."

"Mrs. Bennett in Room 310," Louisa answered, still speaking too loudly.

"Enter." A click signaled Kevin to push the right door, which now opened before them.

As they walked the silent hall toward Room 310, Kevin saw Daniel and Halley coming out.

"Hey!" Daniel said in excited, but hushed tones. The brothers embraced each other and then Daniel and Halley exchanged hugs all around. "I was just going to take Halley back to class. She has a four o'clock lab she really shouldn't miss. The others are in the room."

"Did Monica and Manuél make it from Tijuana?" Kevin asked.

"Monica is here with the kids, but Manuél had a bit of visa trouble. She said he should be here by tomorrow."

"Oh, good."

"I'll be right back after I drop her off," Daniel said as he and Halley headed toward the large metal doors.

Kevin nodded and then led his family into the room where smiles and warm hugs greeted them. Monica, who he always thought of as child-like, now looked old to him, despite that he had a good three years on her. Her son, Angel, appeared nearly a man and Charity, who he remembered as a talkative, zany little girl, had become a somewhat shy pre-teen. Perhaps she would open up later when they gathered at Daniel's house this evening.

They all just needed time—time to get reacquainted, time to adjust to the fear and the sorrow and, maybe, time to say goodbye to a mother and grandmother. But as he finally allowed his gaze to settle on the still form of his mother, lying unconscious on the firm hospital bed, he knew he wasn't ready.

☾   ☾   ☾   ☾   ☾

It felt late—very late, or very early. She couldn't be sure. Amy rolled over to her left side again, unable to get comfortable, not used to sleeping alone. Peering up at the clock by the bed, she made out 2:36. In only four and a half more hours she would have to get up and get the kids ready for school. Only four and a half hours of sleep tonight—if she fell asleep right now.

Minutes melted, leaving no residue behind by which to calm her. Three am came and went. So many thoughts, questions, and torments ran through her mind. How she longed for rest! She longed for even a moment's reprieve from the anger, the hurt, and the guilt. But, eventually, Amy swung a leg over the edge of the bed with a sigh and pulled herself to a seated position. Sleep didn't seem to be an option.

Rising, she made her way to the kitchen, poured herself a mug of milk, and warmed it in the microwave. Moments later she sat in the living room, sipping and trying to focus her mind only on the taste of the warm liquid, on the feel of it as it slid down her throat, and on the tic-tic of the clock on the wall—a sound that, like magic, disappeared during the day, but now made itself known in the stillness of the house.

Sometime later, her bed beckoned again. She climbed under the covers. The clock mercilessly told her it was 4:14. She snuggled down and closed her eyes. Each time she relaxed, her mind went to the argument she had with her husband on that night—the night he had told her about Darla, the night he had told her he was leaving. Her mind replayed it again and again until she feared it might drive her mad. But finally, in sleepy fitfulness, she drifted into an unreal world—a world of conflict and sadness, a world full of problems she couldn't fix. Even as she slipped into a deeper sleep, she had a thought.

God, give me rest. Please! Just give me rest!

Amy walked through a thick fog. White and gray mist licked at naked arms, chilling them. Smoky wisps circled her frozen ankles. Her feet shuffled and crunched dry leaves as she walked. She became aware, without the need to look, that she wore pumps, a skirt, and a silk shirt—as if she had dressed for an interview. But she did notice, with relief, that she also carried a sweater. Amy pulled it on and tugged it tightly across her chest. Some warmth returned. Still, the cool air trailed fingers of chilled fog up around her bare legs and brushed her thighs.

Where am I?

The fog began to clear, and Amy found herself looking over a hilltop park. At least, that is how it appeared. As she glanced around, it changed somehow. It faded in and out; the color and depth meandered. Sometimes she saw it in color and then something shifted and the world became an embossed black and white photograph, of which she formed a part. The hilltop lay bare and flat, except for a few large trees and a single park bench made of carved stone. On the bench sat a woman.

Amy approached, drawing the woman's eyes. In them, Amy noted open curiosity that mirrored her own. Amy smiled.

Is this who I dressed up for?

The woman half-smiled back, muscles pulling in short bursts at the corners of her mouth, revealing hesitance brought on by confusion.

Stiff-backed and perched on the edge of the frozen bench, Amy's new friend sat like an antique porcelain doll, knees together, legs together, hands in her lap. Her only motion, besides turning her head and smiling, was to rub her hands together—but whether she acted out of worry or in response to the chilled air, Amy did not know.

Strangers to this place, the two of them—of this Amy felt certain. While everything else continued to shift from black and white, to color and back again, this woman remained colorless. Everything about her harkened back to an age past—hard-sided, black shoes sprouted legs covered by opaque stockings. She wore a thick, sleeveless and collarless pinafore beneath a thin sweater. A dark, velvet hat sat primly on her head, sporting a half-veil made of black tulle below a row of black rhinestones.

Despite her old-fashioned clothing and manners, she looked young, tidy, and attractive. Amy neared her now and guessed the woman to be about her own age—maybe even younger.

"Hello. I'm Gracie," the lady smiled, looking up to her. She scooted over and asked, "Would you like to sit?"

"Alright." Amy sat next to her and allowed a moment of silence to pass. There seemed to be no hurry here. "Were you waiting for me?"

"I don't... I don't know, really. But I think I'm waiting for someone."

Amy felt she understood the nature of the woman's confusion. Amy didn't know her purpose for being here either, but apparently this lack of understanding bothered the old-fashioned girl far more than it bothered her. In fact, Amy kind-of liked having a moment to sit and rest. No pressure existed for her here—no rush to do anything or fix anything.

"I'm Amy. It's nice to meet you." Amy extended her hand, and Gracie shook it warmly.

Another moment of silence slipped away.

"You know, I don't think you have to worry about whoever you're supposed to meet," Amy said, trying to comfort her. "I'm sure they'll show up eventually."

"Yes.... Perhaps you're right." Gracie paused and then added, "I guess the truth is I'm not sure if I want him to show up yet.... But I'm rather surprised he hasn't."

"I don't think I understand."

"Well, neither do I, but I guess I thought I would meet a man here—or somewhere like this—and he would be waiting for me when I got here. But he isn't. So, I've been waiting for a while now and... well, I guess I just thought I wouldn't have to wait at all."

"Is this man your husband?" Amy asked, wondering if this woman could be old enough to be married. Yes, probably so.

"No. At least, I don't think it would be him." Then Gracie's face changed with the thought. A light came into her eyes. "But wouldn't it be nice if it was?" With this last, she spoke more to herself than to Amy. "I wonder if it will be him!"

"I'm sure he'll come soon—whoever it is."

Gracie looked back at Amy. "Yes... but what about you? Why are you here?"

"I really don't know. And, honestly, I don't care. It's nice here." A little breeze picked up and she pulled her sweater tighter. "At least, it would be nice here if it were a tad warmer."

"Yes. It is a little too chilly for my taste, as well."

Gracie then looked over and picked up a thick shawl. Had it been there before? Amy couldn't remember. But the shawl, a light pink, turned instantly gray at Gracie's touch. Not seeming to notice, Amy's new friend pulled the shawl across her shoulders and down so her brooch barely peeked out over the edges of it.

"I should've brought a jacket instead of this thin sweater," Amy smiled, trying to ignore the oddity of both this place and her new companion.

"Is that it?" Gracie pointed behind Amy to the opposite side of the bench.

Amy turned to see her warm, fur-lined denim jacket on the bench next to her. "How did that—? ...Hmm." She picked it up with careful, suspicious fingers. It felt real—or, at least, real enough. Slipping it over her sweater, she noted that it remained blue. "That's better," she said.

Gracie smiled—a warm and satisfied smile that warmed her face, like that of a mother feeling warmed by having her child add extra layers.

"You're right about it being nice here," she said. "At least, it's nice now that you showed up. I wanted someone to keep me company."

"Tell me," Amy asked, "why are you in such a hurry to leave?"

"I guess because there's still so much to do. I have children who need me and there's work to be done—"

"You have children?" Amy knew she shouldn't interrupt, but she couldn't contain her surprise that this young lady already had children. One child, maybe, but more than one?

"Oh, yes! I have three grown children and they have families of their own, now."

Amy's surprise must have displayed blatantly across her face because Gracie stopped and gave her a curious look. "But you're so young! How could you have three grown children—and grandchildren?"

Gracie smiled as though she didn't understand the question. "Oh, I assure you, I have three children. And they all have children, too. I don't have any great-grandchildren yet. But I hope to still get a chance to meet them one day. If I could just find my way out of here, maybe I could. But the fog is so thick…."

Amy still wondered at the oddity of Gracie's statement, but perhaps in this place time worked differently somehow. What did it really matter anyway? Gracie had trailed off and sat staring into the thick colorless fog that billowed at the edge of the park.

"Is the fog holding you here?" Amy asked.

"I think so… At least, when I tried to get out, I just got turned around and found myself back here."

"Do you want me to help you?" Amy asked, but secretly hoped her offer would be turned down. Amy really had no desire to find the way out. But, to her disappointment, Gracie nodded and smiled thankfully. They stood and began to walk across the dry leaves toward the edge of the park.

"I think it's fall here," Gracie said, but her voice sounded muffled in the midst of a new and very strange sound. It took a moment, but Amy recognized the noise as a distant buzzing—one of the most annoying sounds Amy had ever heard. Gracie began to say something else, but now Amy couldn't make out a single word.

"What?" Amy asked, unable to make out even her own voice over the noise. "What did you say?"

Gracie's face faded, obscured by mist.

"Do you hear that?" Amy said far too loudly, hands moving to her ears. Where did the noise come from?

And then Gracie face contorted in renewed confusion and she shook her head, evidently unable to hear anything out of the ordinary. Gracie stopped walking but, though they had been elbow to elbow a moment ago, she now moved farther and farther away. Soon Amy couldn't reach her, even with arms outstretched. What was happening?

The fog swirl around her, blocking Gracie from sight—but the edge of the park yet lay at some distance. The sound grew louder and louder. Why didn't it stop?

Amy went to cover her ears but found she could only move one of her arms. The other was useless, dead. She squeezed her eyes against the noise, but when she opened them again, the park, the fog, and Gracie had vanished. Her covers rose in billows about her face, her breath gasped from her nose as she attempted to regain wakeful breathing patterns. One arm ached, pinned uncomfortably beneath her. The alarm blared.

❧ Chapter Four ❧

"I've got pepperoni and sausage, a Hawaiian, a cheese only, and who ordered the Quizno's southwestern chicken sub?" Daniel had just returned from making the rounds downtown fulfilling various lunch requests. He stood in the doorway of the small ICU waiting room, pizzas stacked precariously on his flattened right hand and the sub gripped in his left. Two 2-liter bottles of soda swung in a plastic bag dangling from his left arm.

"Oh, that's mine," Celia said.

Angel, entrenched in his skateboarding magazine, perked up with the announcement of food. The smell of the warm pizzas enticed his mouth into a watery state, moving him into an instant, ravenous hunger. But then, he existed in some degree of hunger.

Rescuing the pizzas first from his uncle's hands, Angel cleared a space on a small end table while Daniel placed the sandwich in his wife's hands and then took a Coca-Cola and a Mountain Dew from the bag.

"I thought we might need something to help us stay awake," he explained as he sat them on the floor for lack of table space. "Oh, but I forgot to get some cups."

"I'll go down to the cafeteria and get us some," Charity offered, noting the grateful look in Angel's eyes. He certainly didn't want to get sent away on an errand when there was warm pizza waiting.

"Thanks, sweetie," Daniel winked at his niece as she headed out.

"Oh," Charity stopped at the door. "How many should I get?"

"Let's see," Daniel counted people off on his fingers as he talked. "There's four of us in here, your mom's in the room with Kimberly and Janna, and then there's Kevin, Louisa and Kenneth. That makes… ten of us. Oh, and grab some napkins, too, would you?"

"Sure," she smiled and disappeared.

"Angel." Daniel's voice interrupted the boy's first deep sniff of the pepperoni/sausage combo. "Could you go get the others?"

"No problem," he replied, vastly preferring a trip down the hall to going all the way downstairs. He left and soon retuned with Kenneth by his side and the others following.

"Should we pray or wait for Charity to return with the cups?" Celia asked.

"I say we go ahead and pray," Kenneth voiced the opinion of most of the men in the room.

"We'll make sure to save her some of each kind of pizza," Angel offered as his stomach growled.

"Alright," Daniel began and bowed his head. "Dear Lord, we thank you for your provision of food and drink. Thank you for this chance for us to catch up with our family and spend time together. We pray for Manuél as he travels today and, most of all, we ask that you would be with Mom. Please, heal her, Lord. Touch her body and work the miracle that only you can, and we also ask that you comfort her spirit. Amen."

It was silent for a moment. No one delved into the food right away as they might have at a normal family gathering. They sat considering Daniel's prayer, as again their thoughts returned to their mother and grandmother who could not join in this meal with them. But then Angel's stomach growled again, and Celia said, "Perhaps we should eat."

Kevin smirked and tousled his nephew's hair. "Maybe you should go first—just make sure to leave some for the rest of us."

Angel didn't hesitate but grabbed a large slice of the pepperoni and sausage. Five bites left him ready for a second piece before most of the others even had a first. Charity returned and Daniel pointed her to the front of the line. He filled the paper cups with the crisp, spitting liquids, careful to keep them from bubbling over.

Monica sat chewing thoughtfully. Except for the occasional, "Excuse me," or "Here, I'll pour you a drink," an unusual silence pervaded the small but crowded waiting room. When they all finally found a place to sit—

on chairs or ottomans and some on the floor—Monica said, "Daniel, do you remember the time you got in trouble for dropping water balloons off the roof onto Kevin and me?"

He chuckled at the memory. "I sure do! I didn't know Mom could yell that loud. I didn't see her coming, either. She startled me so bad I almost fell!"

"Sounds like fun!" Kenneth said. "Why did she get so mad?"

"Probably because it was so dangerous," Celia said.

"I think it actually had more to do with the fact that we were on our way to church," Kevin said, remembering. "He missed me, but one of the balloons landed right at Monica's feet and splashed mud up her tights and all over her white dress." He laughed. "How old were you then?"

"About four, I think," Monica answered.

"You can remember that far back?" Louisa asked, surprised.

"Well, Dad died shortly after that."

A short pause followed. Then Kevin said, "Yeah… I remember that summer. I was seven years old. Daniel was already fifteen—and a real pain, as I recall."

"And far too old to be up to that kind of nonsense," Celia observed with mock rebuke.

Daniel only chuckled and then sighed. "I have to admit, I was a rather difficult teenager."

"I find that hard to believe," Kenneth said.

"Believe it," Celia answered, already having heard most of the stories. "But after his dad died, he shaped up. He had to. He was suddenly the man of the house. And he's been a perfect gentleman ever since." She smiled warmly in her husband's general direction.

"Wow!" Louisa commented. "I bet that was hard on your mother—losing her husband and then having to raise you three kids by herself. And all of you at such varied ages."

"I'm sure it wasn't easy," Kevin agreed.

"But she had an incredible faith in God," Monica said to no one in particular. "I've always admired her and looked up to her for that."

"You have that same faith, too," Kimberly said, speaking up for the first time. Kimberly, Daniel's twelve-year-old, never had trouble speaking up in public. This she typically did with a matter-of-factness and shamelessness most adults lack. Thankfully, she usually managed to tell the difference between appropriate comments and inappropriate ones, and speak accordingly. "You always have—for as long as I can remember, anyway."

"Thank you, sweetheart!" Monica smiled and her eyes looked shiny. "That means a lot to me... But, to be honest, I've been wondering, lately... just how my faith is going to hold out through all this. I never expected... I mean, I never thought I would have to say goodbye to her so soon—and not like this!" The tears spilled over unapologetically from her eyes. Now, on the second day of their vigil at their mother's bedside, tears had lost both novelty and need for excuse.

"We may not have to say goodbye at all," Kevin answered. "Dr. Riley said the dialysis is going well. She could wake up at any time."

A moment of silence passed. No one agreed nor disagreed.

"We just need to keep praying," Daniel, meeting nods of agreement.

"It's just hard to see her in there—completely unaware of us!" Monica said and sniffed.

"She certainly would love to see so many of us here together," Celia observed. "Manuél gets here this afternoon, right?"

"Yes," Monica answered. "I'll be so glad when he does."

"Me, too," Charity added.

"And then Halley will be back from her classes about the same time," Celia said. Despite Halley's reluctance to return to class, her parents had insisted she go, promising to text her of any significant change in her grandmother's condition. "What about Clark, Louisa?"

"I talked to him this morning. He finally found a flight, but won't get here until tomorrow evening," Louisa answered. Clark, their oldest son and a graduate student, studied chemical engineering at the University of Florida. "He said he talked to his advisor and got permission to take a week off. Did I tell you he's thinking of going for his doctorate instead of his master's?"

"What do you mean?" Daniel asked.

"He's going to take the doctoral qualifying exam and see if he can convert the work he's done toward a master's into research for a doctorate, instead," Kevin answered.

"You mean skip his master's degree?" Daniel was surprised. "Can you do that?"

"For a nerd, anything is possible," Kenneth said dryly, not even looking up from the back-issue *Sports Illustrated* magazine he perused.

"Kenneth!" Louisa hissed, but was ignored.

"Sure—if you can pass the qualifying exam and you have the support of your department and your advisor," Kevin explained.

"Impressive!" Daniel's eyes widened and his eyebrows rose in admiration.

"How old is he now?" Janna, a tall, slender girl with strawberry blonde hair, wanted to know. She had finished her pizza and rose from her spot on the floor to throw away her greasy napkin in the small, wicker wastebasket by the door. Though her complexion was redder than she would have liked, she had soft, gentle eyes only rivaled by a thinly veiled layer of mischievousness. At nineteen she worked part-time at WISH Medical—a Christian, non-profit pregnancy and STD clinic. She wanted to experience a little bit of life and "give something back" before deciding on her college career path.

"He's twenty-four," Kevin answered. "He'll be twenty-five in May."

"Is he engaged or anything like that?" she asked as she took her place again.

"Not yet."

"Who has time for women when all you do is study?" Kenneth observed, still looking at his magazine.

"What about you?" Janna turned the question on Kenneth. "Do you have a girlfriend?"

At that Kenneth glanced up briefly with a somewhat sheepish look. He paused, cleared his throat and then said, "I'm just trying to pick the best candidate from the large pile of applicants for the position."

At that the others snickered and voiced their doubt about how large this pile really was. Monica glanced from face to face, tears now gone, and found herself laughing at the ribbing her skinny, rather obnoxious nephew had brought on himself. From what she remembered of him, he certainly deserved it and even encouraged it.

She smiled. It felt good to be able to get to know her family again. Three years was a long time to be away. Time had manifested some amazing changes in her nieces and nephews. The youths she remembered had grown into young men and women. She wondered what Clark would be like when he came. He had always been a studious boy—intelligent and intrinsically motivated. In that way, he was quite unlike his younger brother, Kenneth, who exhibited zero interest in furthering his education or even in getting a job, although she knew Kevin was trying to prod him into action. Kenneth was twenty-one years old. He had completed a two-year degree in auto mechanics, but hadn't exactly excelled at it. Now he seemed content to live with his parents, Kevin and Louisa, and let them provide for him.

Monica glanced at Janna, who now listened to another story her father was telling about finding a nest of wasps in their backyard when they were kids and the foolish mischief and mishaps that followed. What would become of Janna? Would she ever decide what she really wanted to do with her life? Of course, working at WISH Medical was a worthy cause and could eventually turn into a career, if that's what she wanted. But Monica was a strong advocate for higher education—if only for the purposes of learning about what the world had to offer, of discovering one's own interests and capabilities, and of learning how to navigate this high-paced, information-saturated society. College contributed more to one's knowing what questions to ask than about knowing all the answers. But one had to go in order to figure that out and recognize the value of it. Monica wondered if Kenneth and Janna would allow themselves this chance.

☾   ☾   ☾   ☾   ☾

"Mom? What's for lunch?" Michael's voice preceded him into the living room, where he found Amy sitting on the floor folding laundry. They had run out of whites again, so she had finally run a load.

"You can make yourself a sandwich," she replied. The past night of little sleep, dulled her voice and made her words sound distant in her ears.

Today, Friday, should've seen the kids at school, but this morning she didn't have the heart—nor the willpower—to send them after the rough day they had all had. So now, Cassandra read a book in her room, and Michael, who had been snacking all morning, stopped playing on the computer to find something else to eat. The clock read noon, after all, and Amy noted with some gratitude that the sorrow that had settled on their family had not affected Michael's appetite.

Amy yawned. Her head felt like it bobbed about in a cloud—a thick cloud, like fog. Fog…

And then she remembered the dream. It came back to her with incredible clarity. She remembered every detail, every word—as if she had really been there—Gracie, the odd clothes, the fading, shifting colors, the sweater and jacket that had appeared out of nowhere. It was all so real…. But it had been a dream, of course. Perhaps it felt real because it had been her only dream last night.

Amy glanced down at the soft pile of t-shirts next to her.

I'm so tired. If I laid my head down on those T-shirts, I'd be asleep in seconds. I wish I could just go to sleep and never wake up.

Amy finished bundling the last pair of socks. They were Devon's. At the thought she immediately regretted washing them. She determined to return the rest of his clothes to him dirty… or torn… or burned to a cinder….

A clatter came from the kitchen.

I should probably go help him, Amy thought, imagining Michael making a mess, and she really didn't have the energy to clean it up or even make him do it right now. *I should probably make a sandwich for Cassandra, too. Maybe I'll even eat something.*

As Amy headed into the kitchen, the phone rang. Out of habit and before she had time to think better of it, she answered.

"Amy? Are you finally home? Where've you been, girl?" It was Idalee.

"Oh, hi, Idalee. How are you?" Then Amy listened to the typical, long spiel about Idalee's vacation, the lost baggage, and how her teenager fell off a horse and broke his collarbone. Amy made the obligatory grunts as she wiped up the smear of mayonnaise Michael had left on the counter and made a ham and cheese sandwich for Cassandra.

"Amy, you don't sound like your normal self," Idalee said and Amy's heart sank. She didn't want to get into this right now. No one knew what had happened—no one—and she wasn't ready for the word to get out. "What's wrong? Are you sick?"

Amy struggled with a response and said finally, "I've just been going through some trouble here, but I'd rather not get into it over the phone."

"Okay, okay… Do you want me to come over?"

"No. Right now's not a good time."

"How about tonight? I could come by this afternoon after work. You could put a movie on for the kids, right? How 'bout I come over then?"

"Uhh… alright." Amy wasn't looking forward to it, but at least it would save her from facing another evening alone. Maybe Idalee wouldn't take up the whole evening talking. Maybe they could distract themselves with some food or a movie of their own.

"OK, girl! I'll see you around five."

"OK. 'Til then."

"Bye."

Amy hung up and called Cassandra for lunch. Then she made herself half a sandwich and poured a glass of milk. By the time she sat down to eat, Michael had returned to the kitchen looking for seconds. Amy suggested an apple, which he took with him downstairs to the computer.

"Don't leave the core on the desk for me to clean up, please," she called after him.

"Mom?" Cassandra looked up at her and swallowed the bite she had been chewing. "When is Daddy going to call?"

"I'm not sure. I thought he was going to call yesterday, but he didn't. Maybe he'll call after he gets h—" Amy changed that, "—after he gets off of work today."

Cassandra was quiet for a moment. "Why hasn't he called us yet? Is he mad at us?"

Amy's thoughts and exhaustion butted against one another in her mind at the question but she looked at her daughter and said, "No, baby. He's not mad at you. Why would he be? You've done nothing wrong. I told you that, already, remember? This is a problem between your father and me."

"So why didn't he call me?"

Amy sighed. "I think maybe he's trying to find the right words to apologize to you. Don't worry, he'll call soon." Amy knew this because Devon would be out of clean underwear soon. He wasn't the type to go get himself new ones. She doubted if he even knew his own size without looking.

"Do you think he'll bring her here?" Cassandra whispered—afraid to ask but needing to know.

"No. I don't think he'll bring her here."

Not after what I did to her.

 "Good. I don't think I want to see her."

"Neither do I."

❧ Chapter Five ❧

"Hola, mi amór."

Monica stepped into the arms of her husband and indulged herself in a long embrace. It felt good to have his strong arms around her again. She hadn't realized until that moment how much she had missed him. They hadn't been parted for long—only a couple of days—but those days had been full of loss and fear. She had really needed him.

"Are ju okay?" he asked rolling his "r" with his thick Spanish accent as he held her. It was a sound she had grown to love—a sound that brought instant comfort.

"I am now," she answered into his shoulder. She sighed and stepped back. "Let's get your bags."

Just after lunch, Monica had borrowed Daniel's car so she could come pick up Manuél from the airport in Lewiston, only a little over half an hour from the hospital. Normally, they flew into Spokane, but Manuél had managed to get a good deal and only paid slightly more to fly into the closer city. Daniel had offered to come get him, but Monica was anxious to see her husband. Now she looked forward to the time they would have in the car to talk before they joined the others.

"I don't have any other bags. They let me carry on this one."

"They did?" Monica looked at his black duffle bag, far larger than the standard size for carry-ons. "There must not have been many people on the flight," she said. Though she sounded surprised, she wasn't really. Strangers were always doing extra things for Manuél for no apparent reason. They gave him the extra-large pizza for the price of a large, bank fees were mysteriously waived, and, despite his bad habit of driving a little too fast and often getting stopped, he had never once received a ticket. Monica might have been concerned if his benefactors were always women, but that wasn't the case.

"Actually, the flight was pretty full," he said.

Monica just smirked and shook her head. If she believed in luck, she would swear he descended from leprechauns. And though the benevolence of others no longer surprised her, it still surprised Manuél, who remained as unassuming and grateful as ever. Perhaps his "luck" continued for this reason.

Manuél served as the pastor of a growing evangelical church in Tijuana. But this had not always been the case. It had taken time for him to become well known and appreciated in the community. As Manuél delved into service among the needy, the people eventually learned to trust him.

Monica, too, appreciated how he served and protected the people of his community, but she saw something more in him. To her, the light of Jesus's love for others literally shown out of his eyes. In fact, his eyes first caught her attention. Because, if Monica were completely honest with herself, Manuél was not the handsomest of men.

Manuél's hair engaged a rapidly losing battle with male pattern baldness, and he stood about six inches shorter than most American men. Monica didn't mind his lack of height, as he still stood taller than she. But Manuél also struggled with his weight. Last summer, they decided to go on a diet together. She didn't need to diet, but agreed to give up carbonated drinks, and he agreed, with great reluctance, to give up pastries. This had been a particularly difficult struggle for him—especially when she insisted that flan—his favorite dessert—did, indeed, qualify as a pastry. But Manuél persevered and had already lost fifteen pounds. Regardless, he remained desperate to lose another five, because they had agreed that, when he lost twenty, he could have an occasional pastry of his choice.

"Are you hungry?" Monica asked as they headed through the automatic glass doors toward the parking lot.

"No. I got lunch on the plane."

"Don't they charge for those now?" she asked, knowing how tight Manuél was with money.

"Yeah, but the lady next to me decided she didn't want the one she got and gave it to me."

Monica just laughed.
"What?"

☽   ☽   ☽   ☽   ☽

Amy realized her mistake the moment she sat down on the couch after lunch. Her eyelids grew so heavy she barely had the strength to push the pillows out of the way before lying down.

I'll just rest my eyes.

Before drifting off, she mentally assured herself her kids were safe and wouldn't need her. Michael played on the computer downstairs and Cassandra colored at the kitchen table.

I really shouldn't let Michael play on the computer all day.

But at that moment she just didn't care.

Cold air still reigned in the park. Fall leaves still crunched underfoot as she cleared the fog and stepped into the broad, open space between reality and fantasy. Gracie still sat alone, straight-backed on the bench looking worried.

"What happened to you?" the black and white photographic woman asked before Amy got within what should be considered reasonable earshot. Amy heard her perfectly, nonetheless.

"I…" Amy paused. How should she answer this question? If she admitted this was a dream, would it all disappear? She didn't want to risk it. She longed to be here—in the only place of rest she had found since Devon told her about—but she pushed that thought away as well. "I just had to go all of a sudden."

"I looked for you, but I couldn't find you. Then I tried to get out of the fog again, but I found myself back here—just like all the other times I've tried."

"I'm sorry." Amy sat next to her as she had before.

"I see you brought a warmer jacket this time," Gracie nodded toward her.

Amy glanced down, surprised to see that she wore a winter coat. She smiled. It felt good on this chilly... what was it, anyway? Afternoon? Morning? Dusk? The sky, a mask of fog penetrated by indistinctive light, revealed no secrets. Time just didn't exist in this gray reality.

"I'm glad you came back," Gracie continued. "It was so nice when you came to talk with me before."

"I enjoyed talking with you, too. And I like this place."

"Yes... You seem to."

"Are you still so eager to leave?" Amy asked her.

"Yes. I've just never been one to sit and do nothing. I guess I'm just not the patient sort."

"Right now that's all I want to do," Amy admitted, going back on her resolve to leave her emotions behind her, "—nothing."

"What's the matter? You look sad."

"My husband..." Amy sought for the right words to use, and then gave up and went with the tired, overused, statistical-sounding phrase she had heard far too often, "left me for another woman."

"Oh, dear!"

Amy saw genuine concern and sympathy grow in her new friend's eyes.

"I'm so sorry to hear that," Gracie added. Then she paused and sighed. "You must be heartbroken."

Amy nodded slightly and then looked away. The fog seemed thicker and darker. Would there be rain?

"When did it happen?" Gracie asked.

Amy told Gracie everything. She told her about the months of suspicion, the fights, and how it all culminated on Wednesday night when he told her he was leaving her because he had fallen in love with Darla—how he "just couldn't pretend anymore."

She unloaded on Gracie about smashing the car, about how confused and hurt the kids were, and about being afraid to leave the house, answer the phone, or even look in the mirror. As she talked, Amy felt the sorrow and the anger and the worry, but somehow she managed to tell it all without crying. A sweet, blissful detachment allowed her a reprieve from the headache of tears. Upon finishing her monologue of sorrow, she felt better somehow—the telling hadn't made the reality of her trials worse after all. She had found a safe place for grief.

When Amy's voice stilled, Gracie slipped a small, warm hand over hers. "I'm so sorry," she said in a near whisper and then paused. "Do you have a church family to go to who can help you through this?"

Amy looked at Gracie. *Strange question*, she thought. "Well, I go to church… some Sundays," she began. "But I probably won't be going back there." *Or to any church ever again.*

"Why is that, dear?"

Amy groaned a sigh, looked down at her lap, and shook her head. She struggled to find the right words when Gracie said, "Are you afraid they'll gossip about you?"

"I guess that's part of it… but Devon goes there, too, of course. And that's where he met D— …the woman," she finished lamely. She didn't want to speak Darla's name—not here where it might taint this sanctuary—perhaps not anywhere or ever.

"Oh, dear!" Gracie considered this new information. "You are afraid to face them again? You're afraid Devon's friends will blame you for this?"

"I don't know.... Maybe.... I guess I just don't see what good it will do. I mean, if everyone at that church is as hypocritical as Devon and Darla are, then what could I possibly gain from it? I lost a husband to them, what's next?"

"Do you really think everyone there is a hypocrite?" Though it sounded like a leading question, Amy could tell Gracie meant it. Was her church full of people pretending to be Christians, or were there people there who genuinely believed and followed the teachings of Christ?

"Oh, I don't know… I guess the pastor and his family are alright…" The more Amy thought about it, the more she had to admit that a large number of the church body did indeed seem to be sincere, whatever that meant. And, honestly, though Devon's betrayal had come as a great shock, Darla's actions hadn't surprised her.

Darla somehow didn't fit there in a way one might expect—even of a visitor. The members had welcomed her warmly and invited her to participate in various activities, but though Darla smiled and shook hands, she always stood a little aloof from the general population. She simply wasn't interested in them. The only people with whom she exhibited any show of genuine interest, Amy now realized, were herself and Devon. Now she understood why.

Devon was a very handsome man. Very masculine, with thick, strong arms and shoulders, wavy brown hair, and a twelve o'clock shadow that showed up by ten am. Darla had been visiting a cousin of hers, who brought her to church, when she had met Amy and Devon there. After that she kept coming. Now Amy realized Darla evidently continued to come because she found Devon more interesting than what the pastor was saying.

Or, perhaps, Darla had been drawn to them because they didn't fit the image of the regulars either.

"How long have you been going there?"

"A couple of years... on and off." Amy paused, but then, for some reason, she decided to tell the truth. "The truth is that something often comes up on Sunday mornings that keeps us from going. Devon likes to sleep in, and so we actually only made it to church about once a month—at least we did until we met *her*. Then suddenly Devon started waking up early enough for us to go. I was glad! I thought he finally decided church could be a benefit for our kids. They always love going to Sunday School and they have friends there. And they were learning good things, so I was happy when he seemed interested. But now I know why he really wanted to..." Amy trailed off.

Gracie just shook her head, but then she asked, "Have you made any other friends there—someone who knows you and who you trust?"

Amy considered the question. "Well, kind of. There's one lady that comes to mind. Her name is Anne. She and her husband taught the Sunday School class we attended."

"What do you like about her?"

"Well, she's funny and friendly. But it's more than that. There's something… real about her. It's like she has a light inside." Amy laughed at herself. "I guess that sounds silly."

"Not at all. I know exactly what you mean."

A muffled sound came from somewhere above them—from out of the fog. Amy started and saw Gracie's expression change from thoughtful to alarmed. For the briefest instant, Amy thought she saw Gracie's lips turn a shade of pink but she couldn't be sure.

"Amy? Are you leaving? Amy?"

Gracie's voice morphed, and the words no longer matched her voice or the motion of her lips. "Mom? Mom, are you asleep?"

Amy moaned and rolled over. Her right shoulder felt numb.

Where am I? Oh. The couch.

It was the middle of the afternoon and Michael stood above her, looking down.

"Are you awake, Mom?"

"I am now."

€   €   €   €   €

The lights still gleamed brightly that late afternoon in room 310. The nurses went in and out periodically to check the dialysis machine, evaluate the readings from the blood pressure machine, monitor Mother Bennett's IV, and so forth. Celia, a tall, slender woman with short-cropped black hair sat in a straight-backed chair next to the bed. The rest of the family had gone back to her home to make dinner and spend time together in more comfortable quarters. But Celia had insisted on staying. She didn't want her mother-in-law to wake up without someone there.

A bottle of lotion rested in Celia's lap. She held her mother-in-law's right hand in hers and slowly, gently worked the lotion into the dry and swollen hand, fingers, and arm. The nurse gave the unseeing Celia an approving look and then said softly, "I'm sure she would like what you're doing."

"Well, it's the least I can do after all she's done for me."

The nurse smiled and touched Celia gently on the shoulder before heading out the door, clipboard in hand. Celia sighed and continued massaging the now warm lotion into the dips and grooves in Mrs. Bennett's wrist. Only the bleep, bleep of the monitor and the soft whirring of the dialysis machine interrupted the silence. Celia felt very alone. She sighed again. She should say something. She had heard that people in comas might still be able to hear voices and sounds.

"I was telling the truth, you know." She said the words aloud, and they felt strange—like she was talking to herself or to the wall. But she continued, "you have done a lot for me. I don't know how I ever would have survived this past year without your help, without your encouragement." As she talked, she found it more comfortable.

"I don't know if I ever actually said this to you before, but when I started losing my sight, I believed my world was over." Celia paused. Talking became difficult again, but this time her struggle had nothing to do with Mrs. Bennett's unresponsiveness. "Even before my sight was completely gone, I went into a dark place where I was completely disconnected—even from what and who I could still see. I felt lost and alone and very afraid. It felt like God had abandoned me." A tear rolled unchecked down her right cheek and was soon joined by a twin on the left. "When you tried to tell me how much He loved me, I resented you. I wondered how you could possibly know how I felt? How could you possibly know how frightened I was?"

Celia's tears flowed freely now. They tickled and so she tried to wipe at them with the back of her hand, so as not to get lotion in her eyes, but her dark glasses got in the way. She gingerly removed them and put them in her lap along with the lotion bottle and used the top edge of her knit blouse. One good thing about wearing dark glasses all the time was that she didn't have to worry about getting eye makeup all over her shirt. She rarely bothered to put any on, fearing clown-like results.

"I was angry," she admitted. "I was angry that Daniel had to do so much for me. I was angry that my girls worried about me all the time. I was angry about all I had lost... I'll never get to look into my husband's blue eyes again, I'll never see my girls' faces again, and I'll never get to see what my grandbabies will look like. People talk about how blind people miss seeing colors and sunsets. I just miss seeing my family—watching their emotions displayed on their faces.

"I never before realized how much communication is done with expressions and body language. I find I don't understand what they're talking about half of the time or even notice when they're talking to me, unless they say my name first. When they forget to do so, I miss things. I can't tell when they're sad or worried or just sleepy.

"And it's been really hard having all the family here again. I mean, I'm glad to see them—I mean, *hear* them." She chuckled at her own inability to break old speech habits. "But I feel left out of the conversations a little bit, almost like I'm not really here anymore. I know, of course, they don't mean for me to feel this way. In fact, they're not really leaving me out at all. I guess I just find it hard to know what to say and even when to say it. I knew my blindness would mean having to learn how to get around and do simple tasks in a new way, but I didn't expect to have to learn a new language, too." Celia paused. She rubbed lotion firmly into her mother-in-law's cracked elbow and smoothed some of it into her upper arm.

A nurse came in and said, "Oh, that's great, what you're doing." It must be a different one than the girl who just left. "I came in to check on the dialysis. It'll just be a minute."

Celia clutched the lotion bottle and the sunglasses and stood. She hoped the nurse wouldn't notice the tear streaks on her face, but had no way of knowing one way or another. "Am I in the way? I'll just move."

"Okay. Could I just move your chair to the other side?"

"Sure. I haven't done that arm yet."

"Perfect!"

Celia stepped aside and heard the nurse moving the chair. The legs of the chair bumped across the tile a few times, and once it sounded like the nurse banged her leg on the bottom of the bed. Finally, though, she said, "There you go. Just come around the bed and you'll find the chair about three feet in front of you."

"Thanks." Celia headed in that direction and felt the nurse pass by her to return to the dialysis machine. Celia sat and felt around gingerly for Mrs. Bennett's left arm, careful to not dislodge the IV needle, before squeezing lotion into her left palm. She started with the hand and fingers while she listened to the bumps, clicks, and breaths of the nurse opposite her. A pencil scratched against paper, and then Celia heard a loud clack. The nurse must have dropped the clipboard and let it bang against the foot of the bed, dangling from its cord.

"Okay, I'm all finished," the nurse announced, and Celia heard her shuffle out the door. She somehow got the feeling this nurse was rather plump and somewhat clumsy. She was nice enough, though.

Celia sighed and again rubbed lotion into Mrs. Bennett's starved skin with slow, massaging motions. The room felt quiet and lonely, but this time Celia appreciated the solitude.

"I guess I just wanted you to know how much you meant to me," Celia began again, in quiet tones. "I never expected to be this close to my mother-in-law, but you've been such a help to me—even more than my own mother, truth be known."

Celia paused, remembering her mother—how she had coddled and pampered and fussed over her blind daughter. But Daniel's mom reacted differently. She had been sympathetic, but she had also been demanding.

"I remember when you insisted that I boil your eggs." Celia couldn't help but chuckle at the memory. "I thought you had lost your mind! Me? Boil eggs? I was blind! Didn't you know that? And when Daniel backed you up, I was so angry! I was sure that could be considered grounds for divorce!"

She chuckled again. "I even told myself you and he had been waiting for me to be down and out so you could team up against me! Do you believe that? I didn't really believe it, of course, but I was just so mad! But I did it. I boiled the eggs. I was almost sad I hadn't scalded myself, too. I was hoping for some ammunition to use against you. But I did fine. And I learned I could do it…. You did that for me."

Celia squeezed a second helping of lotion into her palm and began on the wrist and forearm. She continued working carefully around the IV lodged in the swollen skin on the back of Mrs. Bennett's hand and taped down for several inches along her forearm.

"And you know what?" Celia continued as if there had been no break in the one-sided conversation. "You were right about something else. God does still love me." Another tear slipped free as she heard herself admit it aloud for the first time. "He didn't leave me alone in the dark. He's here with me. In some ways, I think I can see Him better now than I ever did before."

Celia paused her massage and stared without seeing toward where Mrs. Bennett's head lay upon the fluffy, hospital pillow. "I guess you know what it's like to be in a dark place, now. …I've been praying He wouldn't leave you alone in the dark either."

⮞ Chapter Six ⮜

"Hi, Dad," Cassandra spoke into the receiver in a sad, small voice. The girl listened for a while, and then Amy heard her say, "I know.... No.... I know...." Then her distant tone became a pained, confused plea, "But why can't you just come home?"

Amy's heart hurt. Should she put an end to this conversation right now?

"No!" Cassandra's angry voice came out ragged, broken, and angry. She suddenly dumped the device on the table, where it skittered nearly to the edge.

Amy watched Cassandra's tearful flight from the room and then heard the distant sound of Devon's voice. "Cassandra? Cassandra, honey, where'd you go? Cassandra? Amy!" At her name, the voice became angry and insistent.

Amy took slow, measured steps toward the phone. She stared at the upside down, thin rectangle for a brief moment, reluctant. Then she picked it up and held it to her ear.

"I'm here," she said simply.

"Where's Cassandra?"

"She took off to her bedroom."

A pause followed through which Amy could hear the sound of Devon releasing his breath with force and emotion through his nose. It made a deep, gusting sound in her ear. "Let me talk to Michael," he said. An order, not a request.

Amy looked over at Michael, sitting in the rocking chair. His eyes watched her intently, an indeterminable expression on his face. She lowered the receiver to her shoulder. "Your father wants to talk to you," Amy said. Her voice did not sound like her own.

"Well, I don't want to talk to him," Michael said. He got up and walked with surprising calm from the room.

Amy sighed and brought the receiver back up to her ear. "He doesn't want to talk to you," she said, emotionless. Was all of this really happening? She felt a strange detachment from it all, as if she were living out someone else's life. She heard Devon clear his throat. An angry sound.

"What did you say to them, Amy?" he demanded loudly into her ear.

"I told them the truth, Devon," she replied, finding some emotion.

"What do you mean, 'you told them the truth'? Are you trying to make them hate me? Is that what you're doing? Are you trying to use them to get back at me? Is that it?"

"You know, I think you've finally lost your mind," Amy began in a calm but incredulous voice. But then her temper flared. "How dare you blame me for their anger! You left us, remember? Did you think I was the only one you were leaving? Did you really think they wouldn't notice their father just up and disappeared? This is big, Devon! This is big!"

Amy pushed the red button and dumped the phone back onto the table. Her fury had returned with blazing clarity. She felt like screaming and pulling her hair out in clumps! She felt like crashing and smashing every breakable thing in sight! An angry sound tore from her throat, but somehow she managed to control herself this time.

Amy leaned with her back against the wall and let herself slide down to a squat on the floor. She rested her forehead in her right palm, but the tears wouldn't come. She was too angry for tears. Her breath came and went in powerful puffs, like an angry horse. Images of violence entered her mind.

How dare he blame me for this? How dare he? How dare he!

Amy knew that somehow she would have to force herself to swallow her emotions and just do what had to be done. Right now, the children needed her. She decided to check on Cassandra first. She stood and collected herself before walking the short distance down the hall and tapping lightly on her daughter's door.

"Cassandra?"

No answer.

"Cassandra-baby?"

Amy opened the door slowly. Cassandra sat at her desk, her head resting across folded arms on the desk. Long, golden brown ringlets spilled across arms and shoulders. Little, muffled sniffles rose from her. Amy crossed the room, having to avoid stepping on the usual myriad of papers, clothes, and Barbie dolls.

"Sweetheart, are you OK?"

"No!" The word exuded anger and pain, but Amy knew none of it was directed at her.

Amy reached an arm around Cassandra's shoulders and pulled her into a hug. At that, the girl's sobs reached full force.

"Why did he leave us?" the broken little girl asked. "Doesn't he love us anymore?"

"Of course he does!" Amy answered, trying to sound convincing. "He's just a little confused right now! He just needs help."

Cassandra looked up into her mother's eyes and sniffed. "We should pray for him, then," she said.

Amy's mouth opened in shock.

Pray for him? Pray for that cheating b—?

But Cassandra's eyes studied her. Amy couldn't let her daughter be influenced by her anger. After all, Amy had been the one to say he needed help.

"I think that's a good idea, sweetheart," Amy finally managed, wondering if Cassandra detected her difficulty in getting the words to leave her throat. "You—you go ahead and pray for him," she stammered.

Cassandra pulled away and said, "What about you, Mama? Will you pray for him with me?"

I'm going to have to stop sending this child to Sunday School!

"Well, I… I think God might listen to you better."

Cassandra looked confused. "Why?" she asked.

"Oh, well… I don't know …because …it was your idea," she stumbled to a finish.

Cassandra still looked confused but acquiesced, much to her mother's relief.

"Alright. Dear Jesus, please help my daddy. Please help him to…" Cassandra stifled sobs as she went. "Please help him to come home. Please help him to not be confused anymore. Please help Mommy and Michael to not be so angry. And, please help Daddy to love us again."

☾ ☾ ☾ ☾ ☾

Michael scuffed his feet but still walked too fast for Cassandra. "Slow down, Michael!" she demanded hotly.

Instead of slowing, he just plopped himself down in the grass of the soccer field. Whenever the field wasn't being used, they liked to cut through it on the way home from school. Cassandra paused before joining him, wondering if he would just jump up and keep going as soon as she sat. But he didn't. Instead, he began pulling out clumps of grass and tearing them into shreds in a mindless way and then tossing them into the breeze. Cassandra joined him and also began to play with stalks of grass and small twigs and leaves, but her motions were slow and thoughtful.

"Why are you so angry, Michael?"

"Why do you think?"

"But Mom said Dad just needs help—that he's just confused right now. Maybe he'll come back."

"What if I don't want him back?"

"How can you say that? He's Dad!"

"He certainly isn't acting like it!"

"Maybe he just needs our help. Mom says—"

"What does she know?" Michael interrupted.

"What do you mean?"

"She's probably the one who made him leave!" He pulled a large clump of grass from the earth, still dangling with dirt clods, and threw it several yards away. His action created a bare patch in the earth.

"No she didn't!"

"Well then, why did he leave? Mom said that this is between her and Dad, remember? Maybe she told him to go. Did you ever think of that?"

Cassandra's brow wrinkled at the thought. But then she remembered her phone conversation with her father. "She didn't, Michael. Dad said, 'I'm sorry I had to leave. I just decided that I need to live somewhere else.' This was his idea."

Michael, though still angry, considered this. "She still could have told him to go," he said, still clinging to his rage, though he now battled doubt.

"Why do you have to be so angry with her?" Cassandra asked, returning to her tears. "You're just making her feel worse!"

Michael stopped pulling clumps of grass for a moment and sighed through his nose.

"I'm just so mad," he said, and the first tears of hurt and loss came streaming from his eyes. He hung his head in defeat.

Cassandra slipped a hand into one of his dirty ones and rested the side of her head against his shoulder, letting her own tears soak into his shirtsleeve.

☾   ☾   ☾   ☾   ☾

"Hey, girl! Oh, dear! You look just awful!"

Amy tried to smile at Idalee's sympathetic insult, but couldn't manage one. She stepped aside and let her bustling, noisy friend in the door. Idalee dropped her purse, let her keys fall noisily on the hardwood floor of the small entryway, and threw her meaty arms around Amy in a big, motherly hug.

"Oh, my goodness! Whatever has happened? You just tell Idalee everything!"

Amy somehow got free of the hug and said, "We can sit in the living room. The kids went for a walk."

Idalee followed Amy to the couch and nestled her robust bottom between two pillows.

"Would you like some tea or hot chocolate? Sorry, I'm out of coffee."

"Oh, don't worry about me! I'm fine."

Amy sat in the pneumatic recliner across from Idalee and crossed her legs. She sighed and wondered if she shouldn't have tried harder to get Idalee to leave her alone. Normally, she would have jumped at the chance to spend a Friday evening with her friend, but now she just felt dull and uncomfortable. But Idalee was a good friend, and though she had a boisterous nature, she genuinely cared about Amy's feelings. She had become like an aunt to the kids and had even been a confidant at times. And yet, this situation was unlike any other trouble Amy had shared with Idalee before.

"Well, honey? What's happened to you?" Idalee probed with surprising gentleness from her cushioned spot. "Is someone sick?" Idalee eyed her for a moment, then shook her head. "No, that's not it. This is man trouble. What did Devon do?"

Amy allowed herself to look directly into her friend's eyes. Despite Idalee's seeming flippancy, Amy found genuine warmth and compassion there. Amy remembered another look of compassion. Who had it been? Oh, yes. Gracie… in the park… in her dream. She remembered it with clarity now—almost as if it had really happened. She had found it surprisingly easy to share her burdens with Gracie—of course, Gracie had been only a figment of her imagination, she reminded herself. But perhaps it would be good for her to share with a real person. And Idalee sat before her, interested and waiting.

❧ Chapter Seven ❧

Amy rolled over for the hundredth time. Each time she thought she'd found a comfortable position, her legs itched or her back started to ache or her hand started to go numb. And always, always, her mind filled with troublesome thoughts of hopelessness and loss.

Why is this happening to me? Will I ever get over this?

Amy also remembered Idalee's words.

"Honey! Oh, honey! I just can't believe it! How could that man do this to you?"

Amy recalled the many choice words Idalee had used in reference to her husband—words that not only cast a dim light on his character, but also questioned his legitimacy. Amy realized that, though she had already been thinking these words about him and even using them when she was alone, somehow hearing them coming from the mouth of her friend only made her feel more depressed.

Devon was a jerk. She knew it. But hearing him called that and worse by Idalee somehow confirmed it and sucked away what little hope she had of life ever becoming good again. And while it had felt good for a while, like she was dealing out justice—Devon certainly deserved to be verbally shredded—doing so hadn't made anything any better.

So what am I to do?

Amy rolled over and a tear dislodged itself from her eyelid and rolled across her cheek toward her ear as she moved. Hadn't she always heard that talking about your problems helped? So why didn't she feel any better? Why did she still having trouble going to sleep? Amy propped herself on an elbow and glanced at the clock. The red numbers glowed strangely, blurred through her tears. 2:19 a.m. Amy collapsed again on her pillow.

"I can't believe he'd leave you after you gave him the best years of your life!" Idalee's words came back to her.

"And you gave him two beautiful children, and you've been nothing but a loving, faithful wife for fifteen years!"

Had she? If Amy was honest with herself, could she really claim to have always been loving and faithful? Well, she hadn't had an affair, but she knew she hadn't always been loving, either. Against her will, memories of fights and meaningless bickering—even nagging—filled her mind. Had she done this? Had she driven him away? And what about faithfulness? She remembered times when he had asked for help or support—or even love—and she had refused because she had been holding onto some small grudge or complaint against him—often something he wasn't even aware of. Had that been faithfulness? No. It hadn't.

With that thought, a horrible, suffocating guilt filled her. Amy lapsed into sobs and soon her pillow was damp and uncomfortable. How had they let things get so bad? What had happened to them? They had been so in love once… long ago, she realized.

"Men are such pigs!" Idalee had said. "Now you know why I never married! You're better off without him, if you ask me!"

It was tempting to believe her. It was tempting to blame all of manhood—all human males for her pain. It was tempting to believe all men where basically unfaithful, evil creatures. But she thought of her own father. He hadn't been unfaithful to her mother. And she thought about Michael. Did she really want to have that kind of a belief about men as she tried to raise her son? What would that do to him?

'Now you know why I never married! You're better off without him!'

Amy doubted men's fickleness could truly explain why Idalee had never married. And despite it all, Amy didn't feel better off without her husband. Even though things had not been perfect before, this was definitely worse.

This is worse! This is so much worse! What have I done? Michael is right to be angry with me!

And the fingers of Guilt wrapped themselves around her heart.

☾   ☾   ☾   ☾   ☾

The hilltop felt horribly cold. The sky had darkened, and it seemed to take a much longer time for Amy to reach the little stone bench where her friend Gracie awaited her. The grass, leaves, and sky appeared filmy through the milky fog, which cast everything in a dull, gray haze.

"Hello, there!" Gracie called through a cheerful smile as Amy approached.

Amy smiled, but she didn't feel cheery. This place didn't seem as friendly as it once had. Something had followed her here.

"Hello, Gracie," she said glumly as she took her place on the hard, cold bench. A shiver pulsed through her spine and she pulled the coat tighter. She shoved her hands into the pockets.

"What's the matter, Amy? Have things gotten worse?"

Amy looked into Gracie's eyes and, seeing the compassion there, could no longer hold back her tears. She hung her head and sobbed. Gracie pulled her into a warm embrace.

"There, there," Gracie cooed. "It's all right. It's going to be all right. There, there."

After a while Amy managed to calm her emotions. She pulled back and sniffed. Gracie handed her a handkerchief pulled, apparently, out of thin air. Amy blew her nose and wiped her eyes. The handkerchief remained clean and dry.

"I'm sorry," Amy said through a teary gulp. "I just don't know what to do anymore!"

"It's all right, dear. You've been through so much!"

"Devon is such a jerk!" she began, but Gracie said nothing. She neither confirmed nor denied the accusation. She just waited. Perhaps this had not been the way to begin. And again Guilt plagued Amy. "And, what's worse," she finally admitted, "I'm a jerk, too!" Again tears consumed her, and Gracie patted her back.

Amy sniffed and again wiped her eyes and nose on the handkerchief. "Yes... It's true. I didn't realize it at first, Gracie, but it's true. I haven't been a good wife to him. I drove him away!" More tears.

"Amy! Listen to me, now. What he did is on his shoulders, not yours. But, ultimately, placing blame—on anyone—isn't going to help at all! What happened, happened. We only have the time that's right in front of us, Amy—we can't relive yesterday. I know this is hard for you. I know you feel alone and tired and scared—but you won't always feel this way. Things will get better—you just have to trust."

"I don't know how, Gracie. I don't know how to believe things will get better."

"Well, that's not exactly what I meant." Gracie considered for a moment and then said, "I don't mean you need to trust that things will get better—although they will—I meant that you should trust in God."

"Honestly, Gracie... I don't think I know how to do that either... I'm not the most religious person. I want to be—but now I'm just so tired! I just feel exhausted all the time. I'm not sleeping well, and it's so hard to get out of bed in the morning! If it weren't for the kids, I wouldn't get up at all."

"It's not about being religious, Amy. In fact, that's probably the last thing you need." Gracie paused and studied Amy for a while. "I think what you really need is rest... true rest."

Amy didn't understand what Gracie was talking about. If she couldn't get rest here—even while she slept—was there any such thing as true rest? As Amy searched Gracie's face for the answer, she noticed something else. Gracie's voice had been a bit... wistful.

"I'm sorry, Gracie," Amy said. "Here I've been talking about my own troubles and I didn't even ask you how you were doing. I guess you're still waiting for whoever it is that's supposed to come and get you."

Gracie nodded slightly. "Yes... Still waiting..."

Amy grew quiet. The sky looked as if it had lightened a shade, but she couldn't be sure. "How long have you been waiting for him?"

"I'm not sure. Time is… strange here."

Amy nodded.

"I still feel like I have a lot to do. Images of my family keep playing through my mind. Sometimes I almost think I can hear their voices—isn't that odd? And sometimes I think, if I could only get beyond the fog, they'd be there waiting for me."

"But what about your friend? Don't you think you should wait until he comes?"

Gracie sighed. "I don't know. I suppose I should… Part of me really wants to see him—whoever it turns out to be—but I just can't seem to stop worrying about my family. I feel like they need me and that I'm abandoning them."

"What do you mean?"

Gracie paused. "Well, there's my daughter-in-law, for one. I've been thinking of her a lot lately. She went blind just this year."

"Oh, dear!"

"Yes. It's been very hard on her and on my son and their three daughters. At first she was so depressed and angry! I just didn't know what to do! I tried to help her realize she still had a life to live… but I just don't know…. I think I may have just made it harder for her." Gracie trailed off, thinking. "And then there's my second son and his wife. They had it rough from the beginning." Gracie let out a humorless chuckle. "My son is a soft, gentle person, but his wife, well… she's very strong-willed. I worry that once their second son leaves home—if he ever leaves—their marriage will fall apart. Sometimes I wonder if Louisa—that's my daughter-in-law—is babying their youngest and allowing him to stay home so she won't have to face the problems in their marriage."

"How old is their youngest son?"

"He's twenty-one."

"Oh."

"Yes," Gracie agreed with Amy's unspoken surprise. "He should be graduating from college by now, but he just sits around and plays computer games most of the time."

"Did you say anything to them about it?"

Gracie looked guilty. "Yes.... But perhaps I shouldn't have—or perhaps I just didn't say the right thing, I don't know."

They sat in silence for a while, watching the fog shift and the sky crinkle with dark and light. The wind blew and nipped and bit them with frost. The ladies shivered and scooted a little closer together.

"And then there's Monica," Gracie said. Her eyes shown with delight.

"She's your daughter?"

"Yes," she beamed with pride. "I don't think I've ever met a more amazing person—and I'm not just saying that because she's my daughter. I really don't know where her kindness and her compassion and her genuineness of spirit came from—certainly not me—but she's just wonderful."

Amy thought she heard a sniffle come from her friend. "I sure have missed her," Gracie added, with a voice full of emotion. "I haven't seen her in three years. Oh, I've talked to her on the phone and we write often, but it's not really the same. How I wish I could see her again!"

"Maybe you will. Maybe that's who you're waiting for."

"Oh, no! It won't be her!" Gracie said this in a sure and yet somehow satisfied way. Amy was confused but didn't press. "She won't come to this place—at least, not for a long time." Gracie paused and then said, "My daughter married a Mexican pastor. She lives far away and doesn't get home much. But she's doing what God called her to do. They have a growing church and they're always helping the poor and the orphans. I'm very proud of her, of course! But… I'm afraid if I don't get out of here, I'll never see her again… at least, not for a very long time." Gracie trailed off again, staring at the thick fog, lost in her thoughts.

"I'm sorry." Amy said, unable to come up with anything better.

Gracie turned back to Amy with a curious expression on her face. "You seem to know how to get out, though," she said, still considering the thought as she spoke the words. "How do you do it? How do you get out and then come back again?"

Amy didn't know how to answer this question. "I… I don't really know," she managed, not sure if she sounded convincing enough. "It's like I'm just whisked away somehow."

Gracie studied her for a moment and then nodded, brow furrowed in thought. "Yes… it was like that, I suppose…"

"Mom! Wake up! You slept past the alarm!"

Amy jolted awake at Michael's voice, causing the garden, the bench, and Gracie to vanish in a sudden jolt. Her son stood over her, pulling a shirt on over his rumpled hair.

"Oh, dear!" she said as she looked at the clock. It read 8:05. The kids had to be at school in twenty minutes. Amy jumped from the bed and headed to the kitchen to make them a quick breakfast. But just as suddenly as her panic had set in, another thought hit her.

I could just strangle that boy!

"Michael!"

"What?" he asked innocently from the bathroom where he fumbled in a drawer for a comb.

"It's Saturday!"

"Mrs. Bennett?"

"Yes, Dr. Riley?" Louisa answered and rose from her spot next to her mother-in-law's bed. Saturday afternoon found Louisa taking her turn keeping the bed-side vigil but drowsiness plagued her mind, her eyes felt heavy, and her back ached from sitting too long in the uncomfortable hospital chair. At the doctor's voice, she rose and crossed the room, noting with concern that his features drooped with solemn worry.

"Is your husband here at the hospital today?"

"Yes. He's in the waiting room down the hall."

"Let's walk down there, shall we?"

Louisa nodded and followed him out, but worry had already crept into her spirit, chasing away the sleepy feeling.

What's wrong now? What will the doctor tell us about Kevin's mother?

From where Louisa had sat—next to the comatose, elder Mrs. Bennett—no detectable changes had occurred. The elderly patient hadn't moved or made a sound. The heart monitor made regular blips, and the nurses came and went with regular frequency, but none of them had voiced any concerns. Why, then, did Dr. Riley have such a dire look on his face?

They entered the waiting room, and Kevin rose from his place when he saw Dr. Riley. Daniel was there, too, but the rest of the family had gone to get some lunch. Daniel held a half-eaten sandwich in his hand. He swallowed the bite already in his mouth, set the sandwich on a side table, and stood to greet the doctor.

"How is she doing, doctor?" Kevin asked, sensing concern.

"Well, I'm afraid it's not good," Dr. Riley said as he sat down on a purple and orange, square chair opposite them. He motioned them to return to their seats and they obeyed. "I've spoken to other doctors here in town, and I've contacted specialists in coma research and a very prominent cardiologist. I wanted to discuss your mother's case with them, and they all told me the same thing."

Dr. Riley paused, seeming to struggle with finding the right words. "I must tell you that what I heard from them was not what I had hoped for. I had really hoped that, once we were done with all of the dialysis and once the medications had time to work, your mother would come out of her coma. I hoped she would simply wake up."

"But she could still wake up at any moment, right?" Kevin said.

"It's possible, yes. But the longer she stays in the coma, the longer we have to put off surgery. And, frankly,

I don't really know why she's still unconscious. Her blood should be clean enough for her to wake up on her own."

"Is there something we can do? Like, give her a pill or something?" Louisa wanted to know.

"I can't risk giving her a stimulant. Her heart is very weak right now. I don't think her heart could take it. And it probably wouldn't work anyway."

"So what you're saying is," Daniel clarified, "if she doesn't wake up soon, we could lose her to heart failure."

Dr. Riley sighed. "I'm afraid so... Of course, there have been many cases where people have lived for years in a coma. But these people, in general, were otherwise healthy. As in your mother's case, the doctor's couldn't find any medical reason for them to be unconscious. The truth is your mother could very likely wake up at any moment. But, with your mother's heart condition, time is the enemy."

❧ Chapter Eight ❦

"Hey, kids!" Devon's voice jolted Amy painfully from her daydreaming back into reality.

What is he doing here?

But as soon as she asked herself the question, the answer became obvious. He'd come to get more of his things—mostly socks and underwear. Amy wondered abstractly if Darla would wash and fold his underwear for him. Somehow she didn't seem the type.

"Michael, where are you going?" Devon's incredulous voice mingled with the sound of Michael making fast tracks to his bedroom. Michael's door slammed shut and she could hear him fidgeting with the lock.

At the moment, Amy sat on the bed in her room. She could hear Devon's muffled voice as he talked to Cassandra, but couldn't make out the words.

Should I go out and meet him or wait for him to make his way back here?

She got up.

I never want to meet him in the bedroom—never again.

Amy walked down the hall and stood at the threshold to the living room. Cassandra sat on the couch and Devon stood near her, talking.

"So, don't worry," he was saying, "you'll get to see a lot of me, and maybe you can come spend the weekend with me and D—"

"Devon," Amy interrupted him forcefully, "did you come to get your things?"

Devon turned to her with an indiscernible expression. "Yes. Do I have any clean clothes?"

"Yes. Take them all, please—even the dirty ones." Amy instantly felt bad for saying it, for at that moment Cassandra caught her eye. The pain etched in her child's eyes was unmistakable.

What am I doing?

Would Cassandra now also blame her for Devon's leaving?

"Fine," Devon said and turned toward the bedroom.

Amy crossed the room and sat next to her daughter on the couch. Cassandra slipped a hand into her mother's, and Amy held it on her lap, rubbing it gently with her thumb. They could hear Devon opening and closing drawers and what sounded like rustling in the closet for his shoes.

"I guess he's really moving out," Cassandra said in a small voice.

"I guess so."

"Do you want him to leave?"

Amy sighed. "I don't really know, Cassandra. I guess I just wish we could be a happy family—all of us."

"Why can't we?"

"I think it's because your daddy and I just made too many mistakes."

"Can't you just say you're sorry?"

"We should say we're sorry, yes… but I don't think that would fix the problems."

Devon came out of the bedroom then and asked, without really looking at Amy, "Do you know where my razor is? I couldn't find it."

"I haven't touched it."

He made a face and returned to the bedroom to continue his search. Amy and Cassandra sat in silence. Soon Devon reappeared with a large suitcase and a medium-sized duffle bag so full he hadn't been able to zip it back up again.

Amy and her daughter watched him struggle through the front door with it, neither of them offering to lend a hand. Soon he returned to rustle through cupboards, probably looking for his special water bottle, his over-sized coffee mug, and various other items he just couldn't live without.

Strange, Amy thought as a new wave of depression hit her, *he can't live without his coffee mug, but he can live without us….*

The room seemed dull and gray. Finally, Devon found what he had come for and walked into the living room with a bulky plastic bag hanging from his left hand.

"I'm out of checks," he said to Amy.

"Oh?"

"Do you have any more?" He was beginning to lose his patience.

"No," she lied. She had just gotten another box in the mail yesterday.

"I just ordered some more," he said, and she wondered if he had called her bluff. "They should be here by now."

Amy no longer cared if he found out she was lying. How long had he lied to her? How many times had he claimed to have to work late or go to a conference for the weekend when he was really spending time with Darla? How many times had he shared a bed with Darla and then come home and shared a bed with her? The thought sickened her! And why should she make it easier for him to spend their money on this woman? For an instant she almost considered telling him the truth,

Yes, I got the checks, but you can't have them!

If Cassandra hadn't been sitting next to her, she would have.

"I guess you'll just have to go by the bank."

Devon's face darkened. Amy watched him in placidity. There had been a time once when his displeasure with her would have turned her world upside down. Now it only annoyed her.

"Cassandra, sweetie," Devon said to his daughter. "I'll see you soon, OK? I wrote my new number on that piece of paper on the table." He motioned to a half piece of envelope. "You can call me anytime—anytime I'm not at work, that is. If you need me during the day, use my work number."

Cassandra nodded almost imperceptibly.

"Do you want to give your Dad a hug and a kiss before I go?"

Amy felt Cassandra's body make a tiny jolt forward.

She wants to go to him.

But then Cassandra hesitated. She stayed on the couch with her mother, tense and unsure.

"Come on, honey," Devon begged. "Just a little kiss? I probably won't see you for a few days. I'm really going to miss you."

Cassandra glanced at Amy. It broke Amy's heart, but she nodded a consent. Devon didn't deserve Cassandra's affection, but Cassandra needed to give it. Cassandra needed her father, and though everything in Amy wanted to punish Devon, she didn't want Cassandra to suffer more. Cassandra stood and went to her father. He gave her a giant hug and then kissed her on the top of her head.

"I love you, darling," he said. "Be a good girl for your mommy, okay?"

Cassandra nodded glumly.

"And you'll tell Michael for me how much I love him, too, won't you?"

Another nod.

"Okay, sweetie. Bye, bye. I love you." Devon gave her another swift kiss and glanced up at Amy. "I'll call later about when I'll be coming to see the kids," he said.

Amy remained expressionless. Devon grimaced and went out the door. From the window, Cassandra watched him get in the car and drive away.

"What happened to the car?" Cassandra asked, momentarily distracted from her deep sense of loss.

"Oh, uh…" Amy hesitated. "Daddy ran into… a little trouble, is all. Don't worry. It'll get fixed."

Cassandra shrugged and returned to sit next to her mother.

"Do you think I'll ever see him again?" Cassandra asked, her voice shaking.

"Of course you will!" Amy answered. "He still has a job in town, and so you'll see a lot of him."

Cassandra sniffed.

"I think maybe I should check on your brother."

"He's pretty mad," Cassandra said.

"I know. He has a right to be." Amy got up and walked down the hall to Michael's room. She knocked gently. "Michael? It's Mom. Can I come in?"

Amy fully expected to hear an angry rebuff or to be ignored completely. But after a moment or two the sound of feet on carpet briefly preceded the turning of the lock. Michael opened the door and stood before her. His face red, eyes swollen from crying, and expression a combination of anger and loss. And for the first time in many days—months, actually—Michael threw himself into Amy's arms and buried his face in her shoulder. She held him for a long time.

☾   ☾   ☾   ☾   ☾

"We're here!" Louisa called as she opened the door to Daniel's house that evening and entered, Clark one step behind her. Louisa carried his backpack, and he hobbled in sideways with his suitcase against his back leg. "He finally made it!" Louisa smiled as greetings arose from various parts of the house.

"Welcome, Clark," Daniel said as he gave the tired-looking young man a brief hug before taking the bag. "I hope you don't mind sleeping on the floor in the living room. I have an air mattress."

"That'll be fine. I think I could sleep anywhere right now!"

"Oh, that's right!" Daniel glanced at the clock behind him. It read 9:07. "It's already after midnight your time, isn't it?"

"Yeah."

"Well, are you hungry?" Monica asked from her spot at the kitchen table. "We have some roast beef, and I think there's some coleslaw left." She started to get up, but Clark waved her back down.

"Oh, no, no. Don't bother about me. I ate at the airport. Thanks, though, Aunt Monica."

Clark came in the rest of the way while Daniel carried his bag into the living room. Monica gave him a side squeeze and then patted his hand in a motherly way. Clark was no longer the gangly youth she remembered. He was taller and thicker in the chest and shoulders.

Could he be lifting weights? His blue eyes were still youthful, despite the weariness in them now. His hair, once a bright red, had adopted a lighter hue—almost a light brown. His freckles—a source of embarrassment when he was a teen—now lent an attractive youthfulness to his face, creating a sense of approachableness and good humor.

He had grown into himself, and the result was a tall and handsome young man with intelligent, gentle eyes and an easy smile. Kenneth looked very much like his older brother in appearance, Monica noticed, but somehow Kenneth—with his many layers of sarcasm—lacked the easy nature and perhaps even the natural compassion Clark had.

"It sure is good to see you!" she said. "You are all grown up; I just can't believe it! Manuél and I heard about how you're planning on going for your doctorate."

The front door of Daniel's house opened into a tiny hallway right next to the kitchen, with the living room beyond. Clark parked himself in the first chair he saw in the kitchen, and then smiled at Monica with a slight, embarrassed glance down and began to explain about how much easier it would be in the long run to just skip the master's degree.

As they talked, Clark's dad, Kevin, came in and gave him a big bear hug, and then Kimberly, Janna, and Halley took turns greeting him. Manuél, Angel, and Charity also came through. Kenneth meandered in last and stayed only long enough to tease his big brother about how disheveled he looked.

"Do you want to come sleep at Grandma's house with us, dear?" Louisa asked Clark. "Your Dad and Kenneth and I are planning on staying over there, where there's more room. There's that queen size sleeper-sofa over there."

"That's fine," Clark answered with a tired yawn.

"I think he's ready to go now," Monica commented with a smile.

"I think so, too," Clark agreed.

"Alright, we'll get our stuff together and go." Louisa stood to find Kevin and her youngest son.

"Louisa?" Monica asked, "Would it be all right if Angel went with you guys? When you leave, he'll be the only boy around all these girls."

Louisa smiled. "Of course. I'll ask him."

"Thanks," Monica smiled back.

Before long Kevin's family had taken Angel with them back to Grandma's house. Halley left for her apartment in town. Monica helped Charity look for her pajamas, which they discovered under the desk in Kimberly's room.

"What are they doing here?" she asked, mystified, wrinkling her brow. "Did you sleep under the desk?"

Charity laughed. "No! ...I don't know how they got under there. Are my socks there, too?"

Monica groped around a bit. "I don't see them."

"Hmmm."

"Are you liking being in here with Kimberly?" Monica asked her daughter.

"Yeah, it's fun! She has some really cool magazines."

"It's nice to have a cousin that's about your same age, isn't it?"

"Uh, huh. She's nice." Charity paused while she pulled her pajama top over her head and then said, "I wish she could come visit us in Tijuana. I think she would like it."

"Maybe she can sometime."

"Really?"

"Why not?"

"Maybe she and her church youth group could come down and do a service project down there with our church or with the orphanages or something."

Monica looked at her daughter, thoughtfully. "You know, I think that's a great idea!"

"It's not really my idea," Charity admitted. "Kimberly said her youth pastor is already thinking about doing an overseas mission of some sort."

"Really? Well, there's certainly a need for that kind of help. I'll ask your father to get in touch with the youth pastor. Maybe they can work something out."

Charity finished dressing and snuggled under the covers. "Well, if Dad talks to him, you know it's going to happen!"

Monica chuckled and kissed Charity on the forehead. "Goodnight, sweetheart." Monica stood to leave and turned out the lights.

"Mom?"

"Yes, Dear?"

"Can we pray for Grandma?"

"Certainly!"

"Wait for me!" Kimberly said from the hallway.

Monica moved aside to let her twelve-year-old niece into the room. Kimberly's hair dripped even as she rubbed it with a large, blue towel. She stepped gingerly on the trundle bed Charity was using, careful not to step on her cousin's arms or legs, and plopped herself down on her bed. There she sat expectantly, rubbing away the moisture from her strawberry blonde hair.

Monica kneeled beside the beds and began, "Dear Lord, thank you so much for this wonderful family you gave us. Thank you that we are all here together and were all brought here safely. Thank you for Kimberly and Charity and for their friendship and for all the love in this family. And we pray, Lord, that Mom—Grandma—will get better soon. We ask you to heal her body and bring her back to us."

Monica paused. Raw emotion threatened to return, tightening her throat to and causing her mouth to go dry. She swallowed and blinked back tears. "Please be with her, Lord... Please comfort her if she's frightened and protect her from any pain. We know that you love her— even more than we do. Amen."

"Amen," the girls echoed back.

"Do either of you want to pray?" Monica asked.

"I will," Kimberly said and they bowed their heads again. "Dear, Jesus, please be with Grandma in the hospital. Help her know how much we love her. Help her not to feel bad or to have any pain. And help her to get better. But if she doesn't get better, God, help us not to be too sad—because we know that she'll be in Heaven with you and Grandpa. Amen."

Monica struggled against tears, not ready for this kind of prayer.

Mom is too young to die! I haven't even gotten to talk with her yet! This just isn't right! This is all wrong! God can't have her yet!

Monica fought to keep her inner battle from showing on her face. She didn't want Kimberly to think she disapproved of her prayer. But did she? Had Kimberly given up too soon?

"Goodnight, Aunt Monica," Kimberly said as she arranged a small hand towel across her pillow.

"Goodnight, Mom," Charity said.

Monica stood then, kissed the girls, and flipped off the light.

"Goodnight, girls."

In the hallway, contradictory thoughts plagued her. Kimberly's prayer sounded just like Daniel, and Monica remembered her anger at her older brother. Why did he simply accept the doctor's word without question? Where was his faith? Where was his will to pray and fast and fight for the life of his mother?

Wait a minute. What am I thinking? Who am I trying to fight? God? Is praying and fasting merely a way to fight against God—a God who is supposed to be a God of love? A God whose plans and purposes are always best?

Monica slipped into the now empty bathroom and closed the door. She needed some privacy. She needed to think—and, possibly, to confess. Was she wrong to be so stubborn? To need her mother so much? She remembered the many times in Tijuana when her church gathered to pray and fast for some need. And she knew that the Bible taught fasting as a method of supplication. But what was the proper way to go about it?

And as Monica thought about fasting and its purpose, she realized that many times she had viewed it and used it more as a hunger strike than as a method to focus her own desires on God and on His purposes. God didn't need to see her going hungry to have compassion on her or on the people she prayed for. His compassion and desire to help would not be bolstered by such an act from her. After all,

God is perfect and so is His love. Fasting changes nothing about God. And so what was it for?

Monica realized that fasting, like prayer, was for her. It was for humanity, not for God. God desperately desires to be in relationship with His people. But, God's attention and compassion need no help from outside means. Both acts were ways to refocus the human mind—minds stuck in the trappings of worldly concerns—on the greater ways of their perfect, loving Creator, and to help them learn to listen for His voice. And so what was she to do? How was she to feel? Where was her faith?

"Dear, God," Monica prayed again. "I'm sorry I've been so set on having everything my way! And please help me not to be angry with Daniel. But, you know how much I love my mother! You know my heart and how it's breaking right now! But I know you love her, too. I know she was given to us as a blessing from you. I thank you— so much—that she raised us to know you and to love you and to trust you. Lord, help me to trust you now, as she taught us. Help me to rely on your power alone and not on my own ideas and my own attempts to manipulate you. I'm sorry for misunderstanding and misusing your precious gifts of prayer and fasting in the past. Thank you for helping me recognize their purposes. But I still ask you to heal my mother. I still need her, God.... But if you do chose to take her home... please show me how to say goodbye."

❧ Chapter Nine ❧

Sunday morning found Amy in bed, trying to go back to sleep. She soon found she couldn't. The warm morning sunshine of early September morphed into chilly breezes and cloudy skies.

Amy had risen in the middle of the night to close her window—not that she had been sleeping. She still couldn't seem to fall asleep before 2 or 3 am. Often it was even later... earlier? Now she pulled the covers up to her chin and tried to reclaim her dreams. She had met Gracie again that night.

Strange... how often I've had this same dream... and yet it isn't exactly the same.

Gracie remained unchanged. The foggy hilltop still floated in mist—colors shifting in random waves. Even the few trees and the granite bench remained, but the conversation always differed. Amy closed her eyes and tried to sort out how she felt about this last one.

"I just never seem to know when you'll get here or when you'll get whisked away," Gracie had said as Amy approached her from the fog. Gracie's fingers fidgeted in nervous agitation, but she smiled—obviously glad to see Amy again. "Welcome back."

"Thank you," Amy said, taking her place next to her friend. "I'm sorry you're still stuck here. But I'm beginning to like our talks."

Gracie smiled. For a brief instant her cheeks turned an unmistakable shade of pink—but just as suddenly returned to gray.

"I talked to a friend of mine," Amy resumed, trying not to stare. "I thought it would help me feel better..." She trailed off.

"It didn't help?"

"Not really."

"Was it the woman... what was her name? Ann, was it?"

"No," Amy answered. "No, I haven't had the nerve to call Ann yet. This was Idalee. She's probably my best friend."

"And talking with her didn't help?"

"Well, I guess it kind-of did. At least, I've told somebody, right? ...I mean, someone besides you." Amy hoped she hadn't offended her dream friend.

Gracie just smiled and nodded, waiting for more.

"I'm not just keeping it all inside anymore."

"That's good," Gracie said. "We all need friends to share things with sometimes. And you can't expect your troubles to go away just because you talked about them with one or two people... but, at least, now she knows and can help you when you need it."

"I guess so," Amy said, not really convinced. "Idalee sure doesn't like Devon now," she chuckled. "You should've heard what she called him!"

Amy glanced up, realizing Gracie probably wasn't the type to appreciate Idalee's graphic descriptions. Amy looked away again. The fog, though still thick, white, and unmoving, allowed the wind to blow chilly gusts about her ankles.

"But I guess," she continued. "I guess I just thought talking about it might... might...."

"Give you hope?" Gracie finished for her.

Amy paused, considering, but then said, "Yes... give me hope."

"And you didn't find any."

"No."

Gracie paused for a moment and sighed. She looked at Amy with a steady, patient gaze. "Perhaps you were looking in the wrong place. Friends help. Sometimes they can point you in the right direction, but they can't bring true hope."

What is all this about "true" stuff? True rest—now true hope? Isn't rest just rest and hope just hope?

Gracie evidently saw the confusion on Amy's face and continued. "True hope can only be found in Jesus, Amy," she said.

Oh, I get it. Be religious and you'll be happy. No thanks! Religion already lost me my husband.

But even as she thought these things, Amy realized the irony of her own dream person advising her to do something so contrary to what she had always believed and lived. Who was she arguing with, after all? Herself? Some memory from the past? Amy said nothing. She liked Gracie, real or not. And she didn't want to risk losing this reality by throwing Gracie's false logic back in her face, so she just waited.

"Amy," Gracie resumed. "God is a God of hope. He wants to give you true hope—a hope that lasts and endures, regardless of the situations we find ourselves in. Hope is a forward-looking idea.

"You know, my Mexican son-in-law once told me that the Spanish word for hope is *esperanza*. It comes from root word *esperar* or 'to wait'. In this country, we usually think of waiting as a negative thing. But hope is the part of waiting that anticipates the blessings to come. He told me it that *esperanza* was the feeling he had as he waited at the altar for my daughter to walk down the aisle in her white wedding dress. There is a special kind of joy in this feeling—even though there's waiting involved. Hope is knowing something amazing is coming. It's also a kind of faith—like the faith we have in a person.

"So, like all faith, hope is based on something else. If your hope is based only in people, then, when those people let you down, your hope will also fail. You will find yourself feeling hope*less*. But when you base your hope in Jesus—in His love and in His promises—then you will find true hope—a hope that will never prove false—because Jesus can never be false."

Amy said nothing.

Who's the real preacher here, the Mexican or Gracie? What is Gracie talking about?

It sounded good, but could it possibly be true? Could it possibly be true that Amy had never really understood what hope was—what it was supposed to be? And if she had been wrong about hope, then what else had she been wrong about? What about kindness and love and happiness? Were there truer, more significant versions of those things, too?

"Here," Gracie said, "let me show you." Gracie extended her right hand toward Amy. As she did so, she opened her hand, and just as Amy glimpsed Gracie's palm, another object immediately appeared on it. Resting there sat a large, black book. Shiny, black leather, accentuated by the words 'Holy Bible' embossed in distinct, red letters. Somehow, the color remained steady, not affected by the shifting, colorless waves of this place, and lent the book an otherworldly prominence, appearing in relief against the black and white photograph of a woman.

"How did you do that?" Amy asked, incredulous. "Where did that come from?"

"What do you mean?" Gracie answered, equally curious. "It's been here all along."

"Oh...." Amy then remembered the strangeness of this dream hilltop. Funny how real it seemed.

Gracie opened the Bible and flipped through the pages.

"Here we are.... Yes." Gracie pointed to a place on the page and read, "May the God of hope fill you with all joy and peace as you trust in Him, so that you may overflow with hope by the power of the Holy Spirit."

Amy remained silent, not truly understanding the words. It seemed that somehow hope was linked with peace and joy—two more mysteries to her at this point in her life. She felt thoroughly confused. And what did it really matter what one little verse said in the Bible? How could that possibly have any real impact on her life? It felt like trying to cure cancer by reading a poem. Ridiculous!

"But hope isn't just something you can talk yourself into, Amy," Gracie continued, no longer reading. "It comes from trust—trust in Jesus—just like this verse says."

Just then a birdcall sifted merrily through the fog from above. This time she recognized where it came from and was able to prepare herself for waking.

"I'm sorry, Gracie," Amy said, "but I've got to go now."

"So soon?" Gracie's hand fell back into her lap and the Bible mysteriously disappeared. Her disappointment showed plainly on her face and in her eyes.

"I'm sorry. I enjoyed our talk." For a moment, Amy wondered if she were telling the truth or not. Yes, she decided. She had enjoyed it. She enjoyed talking to Gracie—and even though she didn't understand what Gracie meant by reading that verse, Amy felt the warmth and the encouragement in her friend's voice. It was good to know that someone cared about her—even if she was a made-up someone. "I'll come back as soon as I can," Amy promised.

The shrill, meandering whistling grew louder, but this time, as she floated away through the fog toward the noise, she saw that Gracie smiled at her through young, very pink lips.

☾   ☾   ☾   ☾   ☾

"You go ahead," Louisa answered her husband. "I'll stay with your mother while you join the rest of the family at church."

"Alright," Kevin answered. "You have my cell number. I put it on vibrate, so call if anything happens."

"I will. Don't worry."

Kevin hesitated at the door.

"What is it?" Louisa asked.

"Oh, nothing.... It's just.... Do you remember how Mom asked us to go to church with her last time we were up?"

Louisa nodded and a solemn expression came to her face at the memory. "Yes. But we didn't."

"No. We had been fighting and so… Well, that's all in the past now."

Louisa nodded again, but said nothing.

"It's just sad that she's missing out on going with all of us to church this morning. She would have really loved taking us with her and showing us off to all her friends."

"Yes, she would have," Louisa agreed.

"Well, I'll come back for you at lunch time, okay?"

"Alright."

Kevin headed away down the corridor to the double metal doors, and Louisa turned back into Mrs. Bennett's room. She gazed on her mother-in-law for a long time, sorting through her feelings, memories, and worries. Mrs. Bennett's face appeared sallow and dry. Her eyelids, had become so thin and fragile that Louisa noticed tiny veins crisscrossing them.

Louisa sat on the window seat several feet from the bed. From there she couldn't see her mother-in-law very well but she preferred it that way.

The large window overlooked the non-emergency entrance and the parking lot. After a while, she observed Kevin leaving. She watched him cross to their car and get in. Kenneth and Clark waited there for him. Kenneth had usurped her abandoned seat up front, leaving Clark in the back. Once they drove away, Louisa entertained herself by watching others coming and going.

After a while, a nurse entered on her rounds. Louisa waited in uncomfortable silence while the woman checked Mrs. Bennett's pulse and blood pressure, her IV, and then the heart monitor. Louisa was glad for the silence when the nurse left, but became bored with watching traffic. Standing, she crossed the room to a small magazine rack to peruse the covers. But as she returned to her seat, gossip magazine in hand, she glanced down again at her mother-in-law. She looked so alone... so lost.

Louisa felt helpless. It was not a feeling she liked. She prided herself on how capable she was—how organized, how efficient, how competent... but now, sitting here next to a woman in a coma, whom even the doctors were incapable of reviving, she felt ordinary and at a complete loss.

Louisa gave up the idea of a magazine, returned it to its rack, and found her seat again. From where she sat, she could see only her mother-in-law's profile and her left hand that lay limply by her side. Louisa remembered Celia mentioning how she had rubbed lotion into Mrs.

Bennett's skin, and Louisa could see that Mrs. Bennett's hand did indeed look smoother and softer.

Celia is so competent, Louisa thought with near jealousy and then immediately realized the irony of that statement. *Celia is blind now... and yet, somehow she's the only one of us who found a way to actually help Mother Bennett.*

Louisa let out a humorless chuckle at the wonder of it, accompanied by a genuine admiration.

What a woman! It's amazing she can still pour out such love and care on everyone around her, even when she's going through what is probably the scariest time of her life! How does she do it? I'm sure I wouldn't be so generous!

A frown replaced her smirk as she realized the truth of that thought. No. She wouldn't be so generous—not by a long shot.

I wonder if Celia knows how much she blesses everyone around her. She certainly doesn't seem to realize it.... I wonder if that's because she's blind and can't see it, or if it's because she wouldn't notice it anyway....

Louisa realized she didn't know her sister-in-law well enough to make a final judgment on that issue, and let her mind move on to other things.

Her thoughts fled back many years to when she and Kevin had first announced their engagement. She remembered Mrs. Bennett's reaction—kind and patient on the surface but Louisa had immediately felt that Mother Bennett was not thrilled with their decision. After the wedding, it had taken many years for her and her mother-in-law to get close, and even now Louisa knew she didn't share the same affection with Mother Bennett that Celia or even Manuél enjoyed. Things had improved between them over the years, but slowly.

Louisa remembered with some annoyance a recent remark Mother Bennett had made, indicating her hope that Kenneth go to college. The remark immediately put Louisa on the defensive.... But, truthfully, she couldn't remember Mother Bennett saying anything cruel or demeaning—it was just a feeling she had—a feeling that somehow she didn't measure up to what Mrs. Bennett had desired in a wife for her second son.

But now, as Louisa watched the slow—almost too slow—rise and fall of her mother-in-law's chest and heard the beep, beep of the monitor, she wondered what Mother Bennett would say to her now. Would she admit her disappointment in Kevin's choice of a wife? Would she describe the woman she had hoped Kevin would marry? Perhaps some demure, soft-spoken, mousy, ultra-Christian woman? Would she berate her for being too soft of a parent? Or would she deny ever having such thoughts at all? And would Louisa believe her if she did?

Louisa sighed. It sounded loud in the still room and, for the tiniest instant, she worried it might wake her sleeping mother-in-law. This was silly, of course, she immediately realized, as Mother Bennett's waking was precisely what everyone prayed for. Louisa sighed again and wished Mother Bennett would just open her eyes, sit up in the bed, and ask her what she was thinking. She wished she could talk to Mother Bennett—honestly, openly—in a way she rarely ever spoke to anyone unless they were having an argument.

"What would you say," Louisa asked aloud suddenly—almost before she realized what she was doing. She glanced at the door to make sure no one had heard her, then relaxed and looked back at Mrs. Bennett's profile.

"What would you say if I asked you if you loved me?" Louisa stopped suddenly.

Why did I say such a thing? Is that really what I have been wondering all these years?

And as Louisa realized the truth, hot tears formed in her eyes. She remembered her father—a Navy man who spent little time at home during her childhood years. When there, he was strict and unaffectionate. Then he had died, and Louisa had struggled and struggled to remember a single time he had actually said, 'I love you.'

Louisa thought of her mother—a tiny woman, but competent and hardworking. Louisa tried to remember ever seeing her mother sitting and resting. All her memories centered on her mother washing clothes, cooking, or rushing about the house on various errands.

I'm like her, Louisa realized. *And I'm like my father, too—in spite of how I vowed never to become like him. I still find it hard to display healthy love... or accept it. ...Maybe it wasn't Mother Bennett who couldn't love... maybe it was me.*

☾   ☾   ☾   ☾   ☾

"Mom, what day is it?" Cassandra stood opposite the kitchen table, finishing a piece of toast.

"It's Sunday," Amy responded with a yawn.

"Oh! I better get ready for church!"

"Don't bother. We're not going."

"Why not?" Cassandra asked.

"We're just not, okay?" Amy slammed her coffee spoon down on the table.

Cassandra's eyes widened, but then she turned and walked quietly from the room. Amy immediately regretted snapping at her daughter. She sighed.

Why am I on edge? It's probably the lack of sleep. If I don't get a descent night's rest soon, I'm going to go completely mad!

But though Amy regretted her tone, she felt fully justified in her answer. Go to church? Not a chance! What would she say when they asked where Devon was? 'Oh, he's probably sleeping late with Darla.' No. She couldn't face those people—not now—not ever! Michael and Cassandra would just have to make friends elsewhere— like school or a club or something.

Amy got up and walked into the living room. The clock read 9:53.

We've already missed most of Cassandra's Sunday School class anyway. It's just as well. She might as well get used to staying home on Sundays.

Amy deposited herself on the overstuffed couch between the pillows and picked up a magazine from the side table. Under the magazine, though, she found her

Bible, still looking new despite its age. The sight of it reminded her of her dream. To her surprise, parts of the verse that Gracie had read came back to her in a flash.

Amy whispered, "May the God of hope fill you with joy and peace... something... so that you may overflow with hope... something... something."

She frowned.

"I wonder..."

Amy set down her magazine, vowing to herself to return to it as soon as her curiosity was satisfied.

"Hmmm... Now where would that verse be?"

Amy thumbed through the pages without luck and then remembered the concordance in the back. It had been a while since she had used one, but she looked up the word 'hope' and found a similar-looking verse in Romans. Even with the reference numbers, it took her a few moments to locate it.

She read, "May the God of hope fill you with all joy and peace as you trust in Him, so that you may overflow with hope by the power of the Holy Spirit. Romans 15:13."

Amy dropped the book.

How can this be? How could I have imagined a verse in my dreams and then find the same one in the Bible? Impossible!

Amy sat staring the strange, black book on the ground near her feet, now sprawled in a mass of twisted pages.

"I don't believe it... This is too weird!"

I must have read that once and just recalled it from my subconscious while I was dreaming. Yes. That must be it.

She smiled and chuckled to herself. She picked up the Bible, straightened the pages and set it back on the side table. Then she retrieved her magazine and opened to the advice column.

But Amy found it difficult to concentrate on what she read. Finally, she arranged the pillows and reclined on them, holding the magazine up before her. Her eyes felt immediately heavy but, as she drifted off to sleep, a nagging thought kept returning.

I really don't remember ever hearing those words before, let alone memorizing them....

"Oh! There you are!" Gracie's happy welcome brought a smile to Amy's face. "You didn't waste much time coming back, did you?"

"I guess not." Amy took her usual place on the bench, glancing around the hilltop as she did so. Little had changed. The fog still lingered and the air felt cool against her neck and cheeks, but the sky appeared brighter and the wind had stilled.

"Well, I have to admit," Gracie said with a sigh, "I'm so glad you decided to join me again so soon. I could really use your company."

"Oh? Did something happen?"

"Well... I'm not sure, really. Nothing seems to have happened. I mean, I'm still here, obviously... but I keep hearing things—voices. But just as I really start to listen, they drift away." Gracie chuckled at herself then. "I guess that sounds silly—'I'm hearing voices.'"

Amy laughed with her. "I guess it kind-of does sound silly, but that's okay. To be honest, I've heard some voices while I've been here, too."

"You have?"

"Yes. In fact, that's what calls me away sometimes."

Gracie looked thoughtful and seemed to be considering this admission. "Hmm… I wonder if that's how I'll be called out of this place...." Then Gracie's face acquired a stricken look. "You don't think that they've been trying to call me home, and I just haven't been paying attention, do you?"

It was Amy's turn to consider. What in the world should she say? It was strange that her dream-friend was so worried all the time. What did that say about herself?

"No, I don't think so, Gracie," Amy said. "With me, the voices just whisk me away. It's not like I have any real control over it. It's probably the same with you."

"Oh." Gracie sighed in relief and gave a half-smile. "So, you think that when it's my time, I'll just float away?"

"Probably."

Gracie smiled again and seemed to relax.

"So what are the voices saying?" Amy asked her.

"Sometimes I can almost make out the words, but then, when I try to remember them, I'm left with more of a feeling or an impression than an actual statement. Do you know what I mean?"

"I think so."

Amy didn't really know what Gracie meant, but she wanted to be nice.

"Like just a little while ago, for example, I was sitting here by myself—you had gone already—and I thought I heard someone asking me a question."

"But you don't know what the question was?"

"Well, I don't remember the exact words, but I think I know who it was—and what she meant. I think it was my daughter-in-law, Louisa. I think she was asking me to love her."

Gracie paused, thinking. Amy said nothing, letting her friend gather her thoughts and feelings into coherent phrases. But as Amy waited, she saw Gracie's face contort strangely. Gracie was crying.

"What's the matter?" Amy asked, bewildered and instantly concerned.

"I just feel so... so... trapped here!" Gracie produced a handkerchief from somewhere and wiped her eyes.

"I'm so sorry," Amy said weakly.

"I wish so much that I could just take Louisa in my arms and hug her! Just squeeze her until her heart was full to overflowing! ...But I can't. Not from here." Gracie wiped her eyes and elaborated, "Louisa isn't the easiest person to love, Amy, I'm sorry to say. But she has so many wonderful qualities! She's smart and energetic and willing to help anyone who needs it—but she is lonely inside, I think.... She needs so much to feel loved. I just know that if she felt really loved, she would find a way to show others how much she loves them, too. But no matter how much we tried to show her how much we loved her, she just pushed it away, built walls, made excuses to distance herself.... Well, that is, with everyone except her children—especially her youngest. She just babies him all the time. I think she truly doesn't believe she is worthy of love from anyone else."

"I know how she feels," Amy said morosely. "Accepting love is often harder than giving it."

Gracie looked at her and nodded. "Yes.... That's why we have to accept love first."

Amy wasn't sure what Gracie meant. By now she was beginning to recognize when Gracie began a leading sentence, so she looked up curiously and waited for the rest. Gracie smiled.

"Jesus first loved us, Amy. He first loved us."

❧ Chapter Ten ❧

Amy closed her eyes and let the hot water course over her. The near scalding liquid made her feel warm and sleepy and tingly. She finished rinsing the conditioner from her hair and stood for a while longer, letting the heat and the soothing waters bring her back to the edge of sleep.

How is it that a hot shower can make me feel more sleepy and more awake at the same time?

Finally, Amy shut off the water. She squeezed what moisture she could from her shoulder-length, thick, brown hair and stepped out of the shower, quickly grabbing her towel. A sleepy groan escaped her lips as she dried her face first and then rubbed more water from her hair. She moved on to her neck, shoulders, arms and beyond until she was as dry as the steamy room would allow. As she dressed, the fan in the bathroom began to make a dent in the fog. The mirror slowly cleared, and Amy saw her reflection in the glass.

Who is that woman? Look at her! She's plain and fat and ugly! No wonder her husband left her! No wonder he couldn't stand the sight of her anymore!

Amy looked away from herself, not being able to bear her own thoughts. She struggled into her jeans.

I've got a fat butt! And look at those thighs! There are little spots of cellulite all over them! Disgusting! I've completely let myself go!

Amy's eyes moved higher to the 3-inch ripple of flesh that hung over the top of her jeans whenever she wasn't standing perfectly straight. Then she examined further, noting her still plump, but no longer perky, breasts. She felt fat and ugly and thoroughly worthless.

No wonder he doesn't love me anymore.

Three tears spilled from her left eye, almost at once.

Ever since I had Michael.... Amy stopped for a moment as a new thought hit her. *My body didn't start downhill until I got pregnant, and Devon wanted children, too.... How could he let me give him children and put my body through all of that and then leave me?*

The anger was back. A new tear made its way down her left cheek, followed by another on the right. And she thought of Devon and his bony legs and his flat bottom and how he had that strange mole just under his left ear. Most considered him a good-looking man, all the same, but Amy was not in a generous mood.

He's not perfect, either. And he's nearly two years older than I am. He's not exactly getting any better.

Amy finished dressing and began to apply her makeup, much more thickly than usual. It was the first time she had worn any since the day Devon told her about Darla, but her cupboards were getting bare and she had to go to the grocery store after the kids got off to school. Normally, she might not even put makeup on for such a trip but this morning she needed to feel better about herself.

As she applied the compact powder, Amy remembered something someone had said a long time ago about makeup. She had been about fourteen years old and an older boy lived just down the block. What a crush she had on him! Tall, handsome, seventeen years old—and eternally cool—he had said something that caused her immediate horror. She remembered overhearing someone ask him what he thought of girls who wore makeup, and he responded, "Well, if the barn needs painting, then paint it." Amy had turned red with the sudden, terrible thought, *Oh, no! My barn needs painting!*

Since then the thought had become just a distant, humorous memory. But this morning, it came back to her as she again yielded herself to the disguise of makeup.

I'm thirty-five years old, and I look like I've lived each year twice.

She sighed, picked up a pair of tweezers, and began plucking a few eyebrow hairs that had strayed in very wrong directions.

Just like my boobs. They can't seem to stay where they belong. Everything's getting lower....

What's to become of you, Amy, she mentally asked her reflection. *What if Devon is out of your life for good? What if you have to make it on your own?*

Would she have to get a job? Would she ever fall in love with someone else? She doubted it. But her mind lingered on the thought—even as she realized how ridiculous, how absurd, it was.

I could change my name. 'Amy' is such a boring name.

She had always hated it. It made her feel plain and dumpy and easily forgotten.

Amy applied an extra thick layer of lipstick.

Maybe I should choose a name like Veronica or Anastasia or Ana Lucia... Maybe someone would notice me if I had a name like that. Maybe I could make a whole new life. Maybe I could forget Devon, get an exciting job somewhere, and workout to get my abs and thighs back to normal. I could send the kids to stay with their grandparents and take a cruise. I might even meet a handsome stranger named Alec or Esteban and have a steamy romance.

But Amy didn't feel like having a romance with anyone, steamy or otherwise. In fact, she knew that, if Esteban showed up at her door right then, she'd just give him a look of disgust and send him and his tight jeans on their way.

Amy dabbed her burgundy lips on a piece of folded toilet paper. Lipstick, she believed, was the single most important item in her makeup bag. Without it, her face looked dull and off-balance. But skillfully applied lipstick made her look alive and in charge—so much different from how she felt at this moment.

Hmmm... Perhaps I will change my name. Why not? If we get divorced, I'll be changing it anyway. Maybe something like Celeste or Jasmine or Guinevere....

☾   ☾   ☾   ☾   ☾

"Hey, Manuél," Daniel greeted him as Manuél entered after dropping off Monica and Celia at the hospital early that morning. Charity and Kimberly still slept, and the rest of the family had either gone to the hospital or still lingered at Grandma's house. They had found a rare quiet moment, nonexistent in Daniel's home since his mother had made her final, desperate phone call. "Have a seat."

Manuél hung his jacket over the back of a chair and sat next to Daniel at the table.

"What some coffee?" Daniel offered, getting up.

"Café," Manuél repeated the word in Spanish with a grin. "Sure, sounds good."

Daniel retrieved oversized mugs from the cabinet and poured two steaming cups. He then found spoons, cream, and sugar and set them on the table before his brother-in-law. Manuél sipped slowly and carefully from his mug while Daniel sat stirring a generous helping of cream and sugar into his.

"You want a leetle coffee with your meelk and sugar?" Manuél teased him with a grin.

Daniel smirked at himself but kept stirring. "I'm used to the gourmet stuff," he explained. "We ran out of it though and, in all the excitement around here, we haven't gotten a chance to get more. This is all we have left. I guess I'm a little spoiled." He paused and then added, "Sorry we can't offer you better."

"Oh, dis is jus' fine," Manuél said. He paused, sipping for a moment. "About two, two and a half, monz ago I got a new... eh... secretary," he finished, finding the right English word. "She ees probably about sixty-five, seventy years old. Anyway, she makes me coffee every day—three cups." He held up three fingers. "Well, it's the worse coffee I ever tasted in my life!" He laughed. "It tastes like... like mud—mud with a leetle motor oil mixed in." He laughed again. "Anyway, she brings me dis coffee an' say to me, 'Pastór, here is your café. I hope you like it.' Then she turns to go—but every time she stops at dee door an' says, 'Pastór, I want you to know dat I pray for you every day.'" Manuél paused and gave Daniel a meaningful look. "And so I drink the mud—every drop.

How could I not? It's like I'm drinking her prayers. ...I jus wish her prayers tasted better."

Daniel chuckled with a thoughtful expression on his face, imagining the scene. He took another sip of his coffee-flavored cream. "I guess this stuff isn't so bad, after drinking that."

"Are ju keeding? Dis is like heaven!" In proof, Manuél took a long drag on his mug and then smiled broadly. "Umm! It's dee most delicious stuff I ever tasted!"

Daniel laughed at his brother-in-law's exaggeration. Then he said more seriously, "I guess it's not so bad to have a bad cup of coffee once in a while." He was no longer talking about coffee.

"No. It's not bad," Manuél said, catching the change. "It helps you really appreciate all dee good ones."

Daniel looked, unseeing into his mug. "Do you ever wonder if it's going to get any better?"

Manuél sighed, thinking. "Sometimes," he admitted. "But one ting I know for sure, is dat life is always changing. And people are always changing. ...I know you go through some terrible times lately. Celia's blindness, and now your mother. But even dose tings dat seem like dey weel never change... dey will—at least, dey weel seem to, because you weel change in the way you deal with them."

Manuél made a wry face and added, "Now, whether you change for good or for bad, all depends. If you rely on yourself, tings weel tend to get worse." Manuél tipped his chair back slightly, balancing himself on the back two legs and rocking.

"You mean that If I rely on God, then He will help me change for the better—so that I can handle things better."

"Exactly."

"What's that verse?" Daniel tried to remember. "That one about how God won't give you any burden you can't bear?"

The four legs of Manuél's chair touched the floor again, and his expression grew serious. His eyebrows drew together as he thought.

"I have to admit," Daniel added, "I don't know if I can bear all of this."

Manuél breathed out through his nose and nodded. "Dat verse is first Corintios... eh.." he paused, trying to think of the English word.

"Corinthians?"

"Yes, dat's right. Corinthians—first Corinthians 10:13, and it talks about how God will not let you be tempted beyond what you can bear." Manuél's eyebrows parted and went up. He glanced about the room. "You know, I know the verse in Spanish very well, but I tink I should read it in English for you, so I no mess it up. You have a Bible nearby?"

"Sure." Daniel rose and left the kitchen. In moments, he returned with a black, leather-bound Bible. "Here you go." He handed it to Manuél and took his seat again. Daniel sipped his rapidly cooling coffee while Manuél thumbed through the pages.

"Ah, jes... Here we go," Manuél said satisfactorily. He glanced up. "I preach on this verse a lot in Tijuana," he said. "You see, people like dis verse a lot, but dey don't always read the one before it. Let me. It says: 'So, if you tink you are standing firm, be careful dat you don't fall!' Then it goes on to the verse you are talking about: 'No temptation has seized you except what is common to man. And God is faithful; he will not let you be tempted beyond what you can bear. But when you are tempted, He will also provide a way out so that you can stand up under it."

"Hmm," Daniel made the noise, considering. "That's not exactly how I remember it."

Manuél laid the open Bible down in front of him on the table. "No... Mos' people don't. We like to think of it as a promise from God dat bad tings—at least the really bad tings—won't happen to us. Dat somehow God won't let Christian people suffer as much as everyone else. We tell ourselves, 'I know I couldn't bear it if one of my children died, so God won't let dat happen to me'. But den, when it does happen, we think God abandoned us, or He lie to us—or worse, dat He no exist at all."

Manuél paused, letting that sink in. Then, he added with energetic hand motions, "God actually promises us the opposite—bad stuff is going to happen to us. He promises dat we weel suffer. Jus' look up 'suffer' in the concordance or tink about the disciples of Jesus. Dey suffered! Dey suffered a lot! In fact, in the firss chapter of second Corintios, they were so burdened dat dey 'despaired of life itself'."

Daniel nodded but said nothing.

"What God promises is not that Christians will avoid trouble. He is promising dat when trouble comes, He will be der to help us through it. ...A lot of people in Tijuana—at my church and in my neighborhood—are suffering greatly right now. Der is much poverty—much sorrow—many broken homes, violence, orphaned children, and widowed women. It is a hard life."

"Yes...." Daniel agreed simply, considering the bigger picture.

"Dey come to me and say, 'Pastór, why are dees bad tings happening to me? I can no bear dis. I thought God said we would no suffer beyond what we could bear.' And so I say, 'No, my brother,' or 'No, my sister, the opposite is true. There is nothing in dis world—nothing—dat we can bear on our own! If we no have Jesus, we could not even bear the leetle tings! And without Him, we certainly can no bear the hard tings. But if we trust God and desire His purposes above our own and keep seeking Him, He weel help us see His bigger purposes and give us joy—even through trials.' Den I tell dem about God's great love—about how His heart breaks when our hearts break. And I talk about the suffering Jesus went through so we could know dis Love."

Daniel sighed and sloshed the tiny bit of remaining creamy-white coffee around the bottom of his mug. "So, I guess that verse is more about temptation than it is about suffering."

"I think both, probably. Suffering often brings with it many temptations and vice versa. But this verse gives us a very wise warning."

Manuél glanced down at the open Bible again. "'If you think you are standing firm, be careful dat you do not fall!'" He looked up again into Daniel's eyes, "You see, dat's when the real trouble comes. Jus' when we think we have everything worked out. Jus' when we think nothing can touch us—dat we have finally become spiritual enough or wise enough—dat we've learned everything we need to learn to keep from needing God so much—dat's when temptation can be the strongest—because we don't expect it. We think we're beyond dat kind of thing. And when it comes we can no handle eet because ees not what we expect—and maybe we no recognize it as temptation at all.

"Dis temptation can be something like the temptation to rely on our own wisdom instead of God's Word, or to try to solve our problems on our own instead of praying 'bout them and waiting for God to answer us. Temptation often comes as laziness or as impatience. It is no always something obvious—like a guy on the street trying to sell you drugs, or a pretty girl hitting on you, or something like dat."

Daniel smirked at that with an expression that said, "Not anymore, anyway."

Manuél laughed, but then continued. "When you are standing firm, dat kind of ting would no really be a temptation anyway," Manuél said. "The devil would no waste his time on dat. He tries to get you first with leetle things—leetle things that are harder to see."

Manuél paused and watched Daniel for a moment, wondering if his English was good enough for his brother-in-law to understand what he meant.

"Yeah," Daniel said after a moment of silence. "That part of the verse where it says, 'But God is faithful'. That's easy to forget... when you're trying to solve all your problems on your own."

Manuél sighed. He sipped the final bit of cold, black coffee from his mug and set it back on the table. "Jes," he said. "Too easy to forget. But with Him, ju can bear all things... because He can bear all things."

☾   ☾   ☾   ☾   ☾

"If you don't hurry up, you're going to be late!" Amy dropped a sandwich into Michael's lunch bag and then grabbed both it and Cassandra's lunch and walked to the door. "Are your shoes on, Cassandra?" she hollered down the hall.

"Yes," was the reply, muffled behind her closed door. "But I can't find my hairbrush!"

Amy turned back to check the clock on the wall of the living room. It read 8:15. "We should be walking out the door right now! Michael! Are you ready?"

"I'm ready." Michael came from his room and appeared to have been telling the truth. His hair even looked combed.

"Alright, here's your lunch." Amy handed it to him and nudged him gently toward the door. "Go get in the car, we'll be right there."

"Shotgun!" he called, trotting down the front steps and letting the screen door slam behind him.

Amy headed down the hall to Cassandra's room and found her daughter sitting on the floor at the foot of her bed. Her face barely visible beneath a chaotic mass of hair, she sat with a dejected look on her face, no longer looking for her brush.

"Well?" Amy prompted. "Did you find your hairbrush?"

"No."

"Then come on. We'll use Michael's comb."

Amy started to turn back toward the door, but Cassandra didn't move.

"Cassandra, come on! You're going to be late."

"Mom, do I have to go to school?"

Amy sighed. "Yes. You have to go. I'm sorry, but you can't stay home forever. You already missed a day last week."

"But all my friends are going to be asking questions. I just can't face them. Not after what Daddy did."

Amy closed her eyes, feeling the exhaustion again in her shoulders, back, and mind. Mornings had never been easy for her but, after yet another night of insomnia, she couldn't handle this right now. She rubbed her forehead, trying to collect herself. As she did so, she happened to notice Cassandra's hairbrush partially hidden among some stuffed animals on a shelf.

"Here's your hairbrush, Cassandra," Amy said, avoiding her daughter's question. "I'll comb your hair— but quickly. Michael's waiting in the car. I have to drive you today because you don't have time to walk."

"Mom," Cassandra said with a particularly annoying whine to her normally pleasant voice, "pleeeease don't make me go to school today."

"Cassandra," Amy said after taking a long, steadying breath through her nose, "you are going to school! I can't have you sitting around the house all day doing nothing. The sooner you get back to your life, the better. We can't just stop everything."

"You have," Cassandra muttered, but quickly followed with, "Ow!"

Amy didn't apologize for her rough brushing. Instead, she focused all her energy on not completely losing her temper. She finished, drawing no further complaints, stood, and handed Cassandra her lunch bag.

Cassandra reluctantly took it and headed to the front door, followed by her mother, who still breathed roughly through her nose. Once they were in the car, Cassandra asked, "Mom, can I tell my friends what happened?"

"Absolutely not. Don't tell anyone, please. Not yet."

❧ Chapter Eleven ⨾

The clock read 3:11 am. Amy sighed and got up. It was no use. She couldn't sleep. Annoyance turned to anger. Shouldn't sleep be a simple thing? Just to sleep? Why had it become such an enigma? Wasn't it a natural part of life? And, yet, sleeping wasn't like eating or drinking or even breathing. For, who could will themselves to sleep? Sleep could not be commanded; one must resign oneself to it. One must let go, surrender, trust.

No matter how controlling or headstrong a person might be in the day, at night that same person must learn to submit to a power not fully within his or her control. Why? Why did this paradox control every person ever given the breath of life? Why did peoples' sanity, indeed, their very lives, depend on regular moments of total lack of control? Could there be something valuable in letting go? Could there be something valuable in learning to surrender to a force outside one's own control—a force worth trusting?

Amy moaned.

Maybe if I got up and did something else. Stop trying so hard. Maybe it will just come. I'll read until I just fall asleep on the couch. It's not very comfortable but it would be better than not getting any sleep at all. Maybe some hot herbal tea will help.

Amy walked slowly to the kitchen and filled a mug with water. After placing it in the microwave and hitting the beverage button, she went in search of a book to read. She found a romance she had started reading two months ago but never finished. After a critical look, she put it aside.

Maybe a romance isn't what I need right now.

She kept searching and found a Tony Hillerman murder mystery, set on the Navajo reservation. Better. It sounded interesting and didn't threaten to reduce her to a sobbing mess. A murder mystery she could handle, she decided.

I might even be able to star in one.

The microwave beeped, and Amy retrieved her steaming cup and put a teabag in it to steep. After adding some sugar, she carried her cup and book to the couch and made herself comfortable. As she perused the book description just inside the cover, she found her mind wandering.

I wonder how Gracie's doing this evening…

Amy smirked and shook her head.

I can't believe I'm wondering how a figment of my own imagination is doing!

5:30 am dawned before Amy's eyes began to close on their own. She rested the book on her chest and was just about to drift off to sleep when she was startled awake by the sound of crying. Amy moaned and got up. She headed toward the sound and discovered Cassandra sitting in her bed, sniffling.

"What's wrong?" Amy asked as she sat on the edge of the bed. "Bad dream?"

"Yes," Cassandra said through her tears. "Very bad!"

"Do you want to tell me about it?"

"No."

"Are you sure?" Amy yawned in spite of herself. "Maybe talking about it would help."

"It was about Daddy. And talking about it won't help."

Amy sighed. "Alright." She took Cassandra's hand and stroked it. "Lie back down, sweetie, and try to think about something else. Try to think about something nice—like butterflies or unicorns or playing with friends."

Cassandra put her head back on the pillow and wiped her eyes on her sleeve. She stopped crying and closed her eyes. Amy rose, thinking she might be able to sleep in her own bed now. But just as she was about to leave, Cassandra said, "Mom? Could you sit with me until I fall asleep again?"

Amy turned back. "Sure, honey. Sure."

☾   ☾   ☾   ☾   ☾

Kevin and Louisa heard a soft knock on Mother Bennett's hospital room door. They glanced up to see Dr. Riley's head peeking around the doorframe.

"Oh," Louisa greeted him. "Come on in."

As Dr. Riley perched himself on the edge of the window seat, Kenneth and Clark also entered from their short visit to the hospital gift shop. The young men listened attentively as the doctor began his report.

"Well, nothing much has changed," he began. "That's the bad news. But so far, she's still hanging on—which is more than I expected. That's the good news. Aside from that, I just wanted to give you a chance to ask any questions you might have."

"What are your hopes for her regaining consciousness?" Kevin asked from his seat next to his wife.

"Well, it's still certainly possible." Dr. Riley said, but his lips pursed in an expression of continued concern. He breathed out through his nose, looking for a way to supply the hope they so desperately needed. "She's already surprised me by living this long," he said with a smile. "She's stronger than I thought. She may still pull through."

"Her heart condition," Louisa asked, "is it still as bad as it was before?"

"I'm afraid so. And that is still what concerns me the most. But at this point all we can do is wait."

"I don't find waiting easy," Louisa admitted.

Dr. Riley smiled with genuine kindness in his eyes. "No. Neither do I."

"What about the bill?" Kevin asked, afraid of the answer. "How much of this stay is covered by insurance?"

"Well, that's more good news, actually. Your mother had some very good insurance. The deductible was pretty high—$2000—but once that's paid, the rest should be covered at a 100% up to a certain amount. I can't remember the exact number, but I think it's upwards of $300,000 or so. Not bad. And we're still well below it. Even if she tops that amount, I think the coverage only drops to about 80% until it hits $1 million. I'm not exactly sure, but I can have one of the nurses check on that for you if you like."

"Thank you, I'd appreciate it," Kevin said.

Dr. Riley asked them if they had any more questions, but no one could think of any more, so he excused himself and informed them he could be reached through the nurses' station if they needed him. After his departure, the four of them sat in silence for several moments, pensive.

"She looks really different from when I last saw her," Clark said at last, looking at his grandmother. "I don't think I would have known her."

Clark added, "It's almost like this isn't really her— like she's at home baking a casserole or something and we're sitting in the wrong woman's room."

"It is hard to believe, isn't it," Kevin agreed. "And yet, here we are."

"I wish we didn't have to be here at all," Kenneth mumbled.

Kevin and Louisa looked at their son, and though they didn't approve of his blunt tactlessness, they understood his resistance. Kenneth had never dealt well with the suffering of others, intimate relationships, or anything that required more than a minimal expression of emotion. They knew—or, at least, hoped—he had true feelings of affection and compassion somewhere inside him.

Louisa sighed. Kenneth deeply resembled her father, she realized. He had come by this emotional block honestly. He had come by it because of her. Kenneth was like her. But Clark... what of him? Louisa had always thought of her first son as more like Kevin—with his dedication and gentle nature. But could it be that he avoided intimate relationships just as Kenneth did? Could it be that she had somehow caused him to lose faith in committed love? Despite all her promises to herself, she had not only become her father, she had passed on his less-favorable traits to her children.

"Mom? Are you okay?"

Clark eyed her with brow furrowed in concern. Louisa realized she had slipped and allowed herself to cry. Tears slid down her cheeks as from a dam break—the first tears she had cried since their arrival—the first real tears she had cried in a long time. She hated appearing weak and vulnerable to her sons, but certain things needed to be said—confessed—to her family.

"I'm alright," she stammered, though her heart felt tight and painful. "I just want you all to know how s-sorry I am."

"Sorry? Whatever for?" Clark wanted to know.

Louisa looked from one son to the other. "I just want you to know how much I love you—how much I love you both. I know I don't say it nearly enough." She looked at Clark. "Instead I've pushed you." She looked at Kenneth. "Or babied you. But what you really needed was consistency... and love. And I've failed you both."

She couldn't go on. Sobs threatened to overtake her as she sat and tried to gulp them back.

Kevin moved to her side and put an arm around her. The boys—even Kenneth—just looked at her with stricken wonder. They had never seen their mother so overcome by emotion—except when it was anger.

"It's alright, Mom," Kenneth offered uncomfortably. "You haven't failed us."

"Yes I have!" she insisted, not to be dissuaded. "I have! And I don't want to keep doing it, though it might be too late now." She sniffed and wiped at her eyes with the back of her hand. After an uncomfortable silence she looked back up at them, having regained some of her composure. Brow tightened in determination, she said, "I want you both to know that I really and truly love you. No matter how poorly I've communicated it to you in the past. I do."

Both boys simply nodded.

Louisa turned to Kevin. "And you, Kevin. I love you, too. So very much." Her tears threatened to return but she held them at bay. "I don't know why you've stayed with me all these years. I certainly haven't deserved it."

Kevin said nothing, battling emotions of his own. Instead, he kissed the side of her head.

Louisa turned back to her sons. "Clark," she said, "I want you to know how proud I am of you!" Her eyes were shiny with tears but beamed the truth of her statement. "You're intelligent and hard-working. You are compassionate to others... but I worry that your true heart is trapped in... in fear."

"I don't know what you mean, Mom," Clark said with some surprise. "Afraid of what?"

"Of receiving love," Louisa answered. "Just as I am."

Clark said nothing, expression blank.

"I'm not saying I want you to run out and get married just to prove me wrong. That won't really help the problem, anyway. I want you to learn to accept God's love for you, Clark." Louisa realized how strange her words must sound to him. Though she had always dragged them to church, she hardly ever discussed spiritual matters with her sons. But he listened now. "God loves you, Clark. And He is much more capable of showing it than I am. Let Him love you, my son.... Though I'd love to see you fall in love and marry a good woman, even more I want to see you fall in love with Jesus."

Clark just looked at her and nodded slightly. Louisa turned to Kenneth, who avoided her gaze.

"Kenneth," she said, voice strong but gentle with no trace of the usual babying. "You can't live with us anymore."

Kenneth looked up them with a shocked expression. He looked from his mother to his father and back again, questioning. "What?"

"I'm sorry," Louisa continued. "But you're old enough to be on your own. You're old enough to support yourself, wash your own clothes, cook your own meals, and even... make your own mistakes." Louisa put a hand on Kenneth's knee to soften the blow. "You know how much your father and I love you. Now it's time for you to discover God's love, too. He can take care of you so much better than we can, dear. It's time you discovered that for yourself."

Kenneth still bore a stricken expression. He looked at his father only to find equal resolve.

"Your mother's right," Kevin agreed. "It's time. Maybe we can give you a few weeks to find a job or get into some classes." He glanced at his wife.

"Absolutely," she agreed. "But after that you'll be paying rent until you can find a place of your own. And the cooking and cleaning starts immediately."

Kenneth looked at Clark with an incredulous expression on his face.

"Don't look at me," Clark told him. "I've been pushing for this for years. And whatever you do, don't invite me over when it's your turn to cook."

At that Kenneth leaned back in his chair and looked at them. He took in a deep breath and released it through tight lips. Clearly there was no fighting this development. He had half expected this for some time. Now he would just have to get used to it. He sat up straight then he chuckled.

"Okay," he said. "Okay. I'll give it a try."

Louisa sighed and smiled back. "Okay, then!" She looked at Kevin to find him smiling.

Then, Mother Bennett's heart monitor made a loud, terrifying beep.

❧ Chapter Twelve ❧

Amy lingered on the couch at the edge of sleep when the doorbell rang. After getting absolutely no sleep last night, the temptation to ignore it nearly got the better of her. But, it rang again and she groaned and rolled herself up to a sitting position. It had already wakened her. She might as well answer. Amy shuffled to the front door, only vaguely curious as to who it could be. She didn't care that her hair was a mess, as she intended to send either friend or magazine salesman immediately on his or her way.

But neither stood before her. A tall stranger with short-cropped, blonde hair stood peering at her expressionlessly through square-rimmed glasses.

"May I help you?" Amy asked the man, noting the envelope in his hand.

"Are you Amy Raymond?" he asked without smiling.

"Who's asking?" she asked back, not feeling particularly friendly.

"I have a registered letter for Amy Raymond? Are you she?"

"Yes."

"Sign here, please."

Amy obediently signed the man's gray electronic pad with the attached stylus and handed it back to him. In return, he handed her a large manila envelope, nodded to her, and made swift, long strides back down the walkway toward his waiting vehicle.

Amy stared at the envelope, uneasy. She went inside and closed the door securely behind her. She checked the clock. 1:10 in the afternoon. The kids wouldn't be home for a while yet. Amy took the envelope to the kitchen table and sat down with it. She didn't recognize the return address, but she did recognize it as a law firm. That was enough to tell her what was inside. Though part of her had been expecting just such a delivery, she had not been prepared for such swift action.

How long has he been planning this?

Amy's breath began coming in short gasps. She swallowed and took a deep breath before opening the envelope. The stack, several pages thick, poured out onto the table. The first words she saw read RAYMOND VS' RAYMOND.

Amy didn't read any further. She shoved the papers back in the envelope and tossed the whole thing on top of the refrigerator where her kids wouldn't find it.

A strong desire to flee consumed her. She grabbed her purse and car keys. Flooring it, she peeled from the driveway not even knowing where she headed. She just drove. Before she knew it, she was leaving town and heading toward Lewiston.

What am I going to do in Lewiston?

Reason finally punched through the tears, now flowing in great torrents.

My kids are going to be home in a couple of hours and their father certainly won't be there waiting for them! He'll never be there! Never again.

More tears coursed down her cheeks. They began to pool under her chin and trickle down her neck.

I've really lost him. It's real!

Amy slowed and did a U-turn to head back to town. She turned the car a little too soon, soliciting an angry honk from the car that had been unwisely tailgating her. She didn't care. She continued back to town, trying to think of a place she could go to get away—to be alone—but there was nowhere. Her car sped up as more feelings of loss, anger, and rejection flooded her.

He's really leaving me! He's really leaving me for that woman! That Darla! That—!

Somewhere in Amy's subconscious, she knew she headed toward a large intersection but, with the exhaustion from night after sleepless night and thick tears blurring her vision, she misjudged how quickly she approached and how little space she actually had to stop. By the time she slammed on her brakes, it was too late.

The last thing she saw was the front grate of a truck through the passenger side window. A flash of sound, motion, and chaos. Pain. Then, for the first time in many days, a deep sleep engulfed her.

☾   ☾   ☾   ☾   ☾

Mrs. Bennett's room immediately flooded with hospital staff. Kevin and his family pressed themselves against the wall to get out of their way. They couldn't see beyond the many white coats and blue smocks that surrounded their mother and grandmother.

"Oh, no! Oh, no!" Louisa gasped as she heard Dr. Riley tell the other medical personnel that Mrs. Bennett had gone into cardiac arrest.

Louisa's cry drew the attention of a nurse, and she and her family were soon gently but firmly escorted from the room. As soon as they headed down the hall toward the waiting room, the nurse returned to help the others. Louisa glanced back and saw two orderlies running down the hall, pushing a machine on wheels in front of them. Louisa recognized it from the many soap operas she used to watch, but didn't know what it was called. It had two large, flat paddles on the front and was used to send an electrical charge into a stopped heart to jolt it back to life. She shuddered.

Kevin spoke in excited tones on his cell phone as they reached the waiting room, summoning the rest of the family. This might very well be the end.

Louisa followed her sons into the waiting room, but couldn't relax enough to sit. Instead, she paced the small room a few times before stopping in front of the westward-facing window—the only window in the small room. It overlooked the parking lot and the main entrance. She stared out the window, not seeing anything.

"Do you think this is it?" she heard Kenneth ask what they were all thinking.

"I don't know," his father replied in an even tone, having finished with his phone calls. "It might be."

Louisa glanced back at her husband. He remained surprisingly calm. His face didn't mirror the intense worry in her own heart. He looked pensive… relaxed… prayerful—even as his mother lay in there at the edge of death. At that moment, Louisa realized the depth of

Kevin's strength—a depth that came from his faith in Christ. And she realized how often she had mistaken his quiet, gentle nature for weakness. But, he was stronger than the rest of them. Stronger than she. And Louisa gained an immediate, intense respect for him.

Thank you, Lord, for the strength you are giving Kevin. And help me have that kind of strength, too.

Louisa turned back to the window. Soon she would see Daniel's green GMC Jimmy, or maybe Halley's Subaru arriving. Monica might come, driving Mother Bennett's white sedan. But as Louisa waited for those familiar vehicles, her attention strayed further to the busy road beyond the parking lot.

She saw the lights before she actually heard the sirens through the thick window panes. An ambulance sped along as other cars slowed and crept over to the shoulders. It made the right turn toward the hospital and careened closer and closer at an impressive rate until slowing just as it left her field of vision, heading toward the emergency entrance to the north.

Lord, please be with whoever is in that ambulance.

She had never said such a spontaneous prayer before for a stranger but today it felt natural. And she determined that, from now on, she would always say such a prayer any time she heard a siren.

☾   ☾   ☾   ☾   ☾

"Gracie? Are you alright?"

Amy approached her friend with fast, long strides. Everything had darkened to a charcoal gray. No colors of any kind were detectable today. Something had changed. Gracie had changed as well. She no longer sat on the bench. Instead, she sprawled on the ground next to it, face buried in her arms, clinging to the legs of the bench as if for dear life. She didn't even look up at Amy's approach.

"Be careful," came her desperate reply. "Be careful or it will blow you away!"

"What do you mean?" Amy dropped to the ground next to her, kneeling and extending warm arms around her friend.

"Can't you feel it? Can't you feel that strong wind?" Gracie gasped and then continued, still clinging fearfully to the bench. "It's so strong! I think it might be a tornado!"

Amy glanced around, doubting her own senses for a moment. But the air was still. Even the leaves at her feet lulled at rest.

"I don't feel any wind, Gracie. It's quite peaceful here on the hill."

"I can feel it. It's going to blow me away. It's trying to take me!"

"Just let go. There's no wind."

"I can't!" Gracie's reply sounded desperate, frightened.

Amy gave up trying to convince her friend of the safety of the place and adopted a more comfortable position next to Gracie.

She sighed. Something else tried to invade her peace. She could feel a memory—a bad thought—trying to surface. Gracie felt uncomfortable in her body; Amy felt uncomfortable in her spirit, plagued by a nameless anxiety. Something lingered nearby—hovering over her, reaching for her—something hidden in the fog above. As this realization dawned, the gray leaves around her and around Gracie's legs begin to rustle and blow about.

"Yes.... I suppose there is a wind, after all," she replied, remembering a manila envelope and a stack of papers. Something about them was bad... very bad. But she couldn't seem to recall the words written on them.

"It's trying to take me away," Gracie insisted again. "I'm not ready. I'm not ready yet."

"I wish it would take me," Amy responded.

Only then did Gracie venture to look up. The intensity of her grip on the bench lessened a bit.

"What happened, Amy?"

"I think everything is over for me. It's all over."

"What do you mean?"

"I'm not sure," Amy replied, considering. Her mind felt foggy somehow, like the edges of this place. "I just feel like I've reached the end of a path and there's nothing beyond it."

Gracie remained silent for a moment, but she still clung to the bench. "I feel like my path stretches before me," she said, "but all I want to do is go back."

☾   ☾   ☾   ☾   ☾

"Mr. and Mrs. Bennett?"

"Oh, Doctor!" Louisa stood up and took a step toward him, her face anxious, mirroring the others in the room.

The rest of the family had gathered in the waiting room to await what news the doctors might give them. Kevin had summoned them all there and they had waited over two hours in frightened anticipation. Now all eyes rested on Dr. Riley who stood just inside the doorway of the overcrowded waiting room.

"Well," he began, "I don't know how, but she pulled through."

A chorus of sighs followed his announcement as the room released its breath. They all watched Dr. Riley's face, hoping for further comfort, but seeing only concern.

"Mrs. Bennett has suffered a heart attack," he continued. "This is what we've been fearing would happen. Thankfully, it was a mild one. She somehow managed to survive it. Your mother has more strength than I thought possible... but this attack has weakened her severely. And, worse, she still has not regained consciousness."

❧ Chapter Thirteen ❦

"I'm thinking of changing my name," Amy confided in her friend as they sat in the cool breeze of the hilltop. The strong wind had dissipated, and the two women now shared their bench, side by side.

"Oh? Why?" Gracie asked.

"I've been looking at lists of names on the internet. I just need a change. I want to feel... different... I need to feel... beautiful." That last word came out with difficulty. Amy nearly choked on it. "And 'Amy' is plain and ugly... like how I feel now."

Gracie sat silently for a moment, studying her companion. "But I think 'Amy' is a lovely name."

"I don't."

"Do you really think changing your name will make you feel any different?"

A tear made its way down Amy's left cheek.

"I don't know. But I don't know what else to do."

Gracie patted Amy's knee—a comforting, motherly gesture. "Maybe doing something isn't the answer." Gracie glanced toward the turbulent clouds above them and sighed. "We always think we need to do something. We think we can fix ourselves—our lives—if we only do more... be more. But the truth is we really can't do any better... at least, not alone."

"You mean I should pray. Ask God to help me." It was almost an accusation.

"What makes us think we can do everything on our own? What makes us think we were even meant to? If God is a God of love... if He's perfect and good and holy... what makes us think we could ever, in our imperfection and ignorance, make ourselves good enough to be with Him? To merit His love? To gain His attention?"

"We couldn't," Amy answered, defeated. "So why bother?"

"Because He bothered for us... by sending Jesus."
Gracie was silent for a moment. "Do you know what your
name means?"

Amy had been looking at the dead leaves at her feet.
She glanced up. "No," she answered.

"It means 'beloved'."

Amy sighed and looked back at her feet. "I don't feel
beloved."

"But you are. You are."

☾　　☾　　☾　　☾　　☾

The arrival of late afternoon brought Dr. Riley's
permission for the Bennett family to see Mrs. Bennett. At
first, they all crowded into the room and stared at her—
shocked to find that she indeed looked worse than she had
before—something none of them had imagined possible.

After a few minutes, they decided it was neither
necessary nor prudent for them all to remain at the
hospital. Monica volunteered to stay behind but first
Manuél led them into the waiting room again so they
could pray.

"You know, I'm not even sure what we should pray
for," Daniel admitted with a glance at Monica. "Should
we pray for Mom to get better? Or something else? How
do we know God's will in this matter?"

Daniel's words surprised Monica. He had seemed so
sure all this time, that God held the future in His hand. He
had seemed so certain that everything would work out
fine, no matter what happened. Why was he now
questioning? Or had he, perhaps, just been trying to
remain strong for her and the rest of the family?

"I don't tink knowing what God weel do and
knowing God's weel ees the same thing," Manuél said.
The others waited for him to continue. "I tink we
sometimes believe that 'spiritual people' know what God
is going to do before He does it—and dat maybe dat's
how dey can 'pray in His will'. But dat's not what God's
Word says. In the Bible, God no always tells His servants
'xactly what He's going to do. He mos' often jus says,

'Obey' or 'Follow Me.' He gives directions and desires our obedience, but He no always share what the outcome weel be. He does, however, tell us what His weel is. His weel is for us to love Him. In second Peter, He also tells us it is no His weel dat any should perish. Now, we know dis verse is referring to spiritual death. But if you remember, in Genesis, Adam and Eve were originally created to live forever. And so we know death has no part of His perfect weel."

"But we're all going to die eventually," Kenneth said, confusion written on his face.

"Yes," Manuél answered, undaunted, "because of sin, we all die eventually. But God also tells us how much He love us. And He acted on dat love by sending Jesus to us—so through His death and resurrection we could have true life. And dis is why we can know God's perfect weel does no include dat we should suffer or shed tears or die. If it did, den why bother sending Jesus to make a way for us to escape it? He could have jus lef' us to what we deserve. But God does not want dat for us. It pains Him to see us suffering. When we cry, He cries. When we suffer, He suffers.

"Right now, we see a mother, mother-in-law, and grandmother, lying in dair close to death. But God sees a child of His who is full of life—true life. If she dies, we weel feel loss—separation. But death cannot separate her from God. Because she is His already, it can only bring her closer. She is no dying, she is coming alive. Physical death, like physical life is only a shadow of a much greater reality. To God, she can never die. And if we believe in Him, too, she can never truly be dead to us, either. For we know we weel see her again."

Only silence followed until Celia said, "You know, I've been a Christian for a long time. And I have gone through hard times before. But when I lost my eyesight I really struggled. I still struggle. I was sure God had messed up, somehow. I mean, I was a good person—a good Christian. I went to Bible study and helped with Children's Church and even volunteered my time at the shelter for battered women. I read my Bible and prayed....

"So, when I first started to lose my eyesight, I was sure God would heal me—that this was just a test, and He would reward me for being faithful to Him. I thought maybe He would use it to show others how the faithful can be restored. When I finally went blind, I felt very confused. Why would He allow this to happen to me, of all people? Had I somehow failed Him?

"But, lately, I've come to another thought—not even a conclusion, really—just a thought. Why should God spare His children—Christians—from pain and suffering? I mean, why would He? He wants to—we see that from the Bible's description of the Garden of Eden and from His promise of Heaven—but why would He do so now—while sin is still in the world? If He did, what would happen?

"All of the Christians would be happy and healthy. We wouldn't ever worry about money or getting our hearts broken. We wouldn't ever get sick or feel tired or anxious. We certainly wouldn't lose our eyesight! But, would we be able to empathize with anyone else's pain?

"What would that say to the rest of the world? That God only cares about our physical well-being. That belief in Christ is about living a care-free life, not about being reconciled to God or trusting Him. People would come to God just to be rid of their money problems or their illnesses. They wouldn't care about Jesus... and that, of course, would defeat the whole purpose, wouldn't it?"

"And the more you think of it," Clark chimed in, "the more ridiculous it gets. For one thing, faith would be non-existent. Furthermore, much of the suffering we experience we bring on ourselves. And sometimes we don't even know we're doing it. How would we learn anything?"

"I can't say I understand why this is happening," Celia resumed. "I don't know why God chose to allow Mother Bennett to suffer from kidney failure or slip into a coma. I don't know why He allowed me to lose my sight. But I do know that, whatever happens, it will be okay. I know God will continue to care for us. I may not know what He is doing in our physical lives... but I do know what He is doing in our spiritual lives. Everything is meant to draw us closer to Him... to show His glory in a dark world. And when He does that, it will be something we all can see."

The family contemplated together in silence. After a while Manuél said, "I tink we should pray for those tings we are sure are God's weel—for peace and for insight into His purposes. For God's glory to shine tough us and through dis situation. We can pray for dose aroun' us to be touched by God's love. We can pray for comfort and assurance as we face our fears. We can pray for courage an' trust an' for rest in Him. And mos' of all, we can pray for Mother Bennett to be free from pain an' fear and for her to continue to live in Christ—no matter what."

☾　☾　☾　☾　☾

Everything looked hazy, outlines blurred and misted. Images moved in and out of sight. The fog boiled about in the sky. But after a few moments, new images appeared within the fog. And as the fog and the hilltop and Gracie slipped away, Amy became conscious of sounds.

Something beeped. Voices came from somewhere out of sight. Female voices. At least two of them. Amy tried to move and found her body stiff and uncomfortable. Then pain. Dull at first but it increased in step with awareness. She moaned and the voices stopped. A second later, a curly headed, round-faced woman hovered over her.

"Well, hello," she said with a cheerful smile. "I see you're finally waking up. That's good! The doctor will be happy to hear it."

"Wh...wh..." Amy couldn't seem to formulate the words.

"Oh, you're in the hospital," the nurse answered the wrong question. "You were in quite a bad car accident, I'm afraid, but luckily the worst you got was a concussion and a broken arm. You also have some minor cuts, bruises and abrasions. You'll be sore for a while. Still, you are a very lucky lady!"

Well, that explained the pain, but Amy desperately needed more answers. And she didn't feel at all lucky.

"My... my kids," Amy managed to force the question into the still hazy atmosphere of the hospital room. They must have given her drugs, for she couldn't seem to come fully awake, but she had to know if her kids were being cared for.

"Oh!" The nurse understood. "They're just fine! They were here earlier to visit you, actually. Your friend, Idalee, brought them, but you were still unconscious. They stayed for a while but then went to go get some dinner. You can call them if you like. I wrote down her cell number for you." She turned and took a slip of paper off the small dresser and placed it in Amy's right hand— the one not bound by a cast.

"How long have I been here?" Amy's words came easier now, but her mouth had a weird taste in it. A drink of water would be good right now. She glanced about and located a hospital water bottle with a bendy straw in it on the table near her bed. The nurse anticipated her need and held it for her as she sipped.

"Oh, not long. They brought you in early this afternoon. I wasn't working then, but I think that was at about 1:45 or so. Then they had to set your arm and put it in a cast." She glanced up at the clock. "Now it's ten 'til eleven."

Amy nodded as she finished her long sip. She sighed, somewhat refreshed from the cool water. She looked at Idalee's number on the slip of paper in her hand. She didn't need it. She had Idalee's cell number memorized. Soon she would get up the strength to call, but she felt great relief to know her kids were being cared for.

"The doctor will be right in to check on you," the nurse resumed. "He's on his way."

Amy decided to wait for the doctor and call later. After ten minutes, though, and no doctor, she changed her mind and reached for the phone. By now she felt more coherent. She punched in Idalee's number.

"Hello?"

"Idalee?"

"Amy! You're awake! Finally! How are you feelin'? Oh, girl, I was so worried about you! But it's so good to know you're finally awake! And don't you worry about nuthin'! I'm with your kids right now, and they're fine. When they got home, you weren't there, and there was a message on the machine from the hospital, so they called me. Well, actually, first they tried to get ahold of Devon, but couldn't—no surprise there!—so they called me next.

"Anyway, I told them to just sit tight; I'd be right there. So, as soon as I got to them, I listened to the message. The hospital staff was trying to locate a next of kin and found your number in your phone. Anyway, I called the hospital back, and they told me all about your accident, so we high-tailed it there. But you were still unconscious. We waited about five hours, and then finally the kids were gettin' hungry, so I took them back to your place and fed them some dinner. That's where we are now. Oh, and, by the way, you're out of eggs. I wrote it on your list. Oh, and cheese. I made them omelets for dinner—hope that's okay. But now that you're awake, do you want me to bring them back to see you?"

"It's pretty late, and I'm okay," Amy managed. Just listening to Idalee made her feel out of breath. "Maybe just bring them by in the morning?"

"Will do. Are you okay? Are you in much pain? The doctors told me about the broken arm. I bet it hurts somethin' awful!"

"Actually, I don't feel much right now. I think they've got me on quite a few painkillers."

"Well, that's a blessing, anyway. Drugs are wonderful, aren't they? Well, we'll be there first thing in the morning, alright?"

"Alright… did you ever get ahold of Devon?"

A pause—a rare thing for Idalee. But Amy knew if she waited long enough Idalee would tell all. She waited.

"Well, I called his office. He was out. So I left a message, but he never called me back. I left my cell number, so it's no wonder. He's never much liked me anyway. So I waited until I thought he'd be back at his new place—Cassandra gave me the number. So I called there and… well… she answered. I told her I had to talk to Devon, and that infernal woman demanded to know what for! Can you believe that? Suspicious already! Well, I almost hung up on that sassy little tart, but then figured I might as well tell her, so I did. Finally, I got to talk to Devon, and he said he'd try to come by to see you at the hospital. But I guess he hasn't come yet."

"Well, I don't know," Amy said. "He might've; but I just now woke up."

"Well, that's true. He might've been there already and had to leave."

"Hey, let me talk to the kids."

Idalee called over her shoulder, "Michael, Cassie, yer mom woke up and she's askin' for ya! Come say hello! Amy, I'm putting you on speaker."

"Okay."

"Mom, are you there?" It was Cass's voice.

"I'm here, baby."

"Are you okay?"

"I'm a little worse for wear, but I'm going to be fine."

"We were really worried about you, Mom," Michael said.

"I'm sorry to have put you through that, sweetheart. Don't worry anymore. I'll be home soon."

"Can we come see you?" Cass asked.

"Not tonight. It's late," Amy answered. "But Idalee is going to bring you in the morning."

"Okay," she responded, disappointment marking her voice.

"Get some rest, Mom," Michael said. "I love you."

"I love you, too, Mom," Cass loudly mirrored her big brother.

"I love you both, too, very much. I'm glad you're alright and that Idalee's looking out for you. Bye now."

"Bye, Mom! Love you!" They said in unison.

Amy put the phone down and leaned back more deeply into the pillows. She took a deep breath and remembered something.

Good thing I hid those divorce papers! The last thing we need right now is to face that.

Her thoughts turned to Devon.

Has he already been here? Did he come to see me? Would he?

Part of her longed for him to come—to prove he still had at least a shred of concern for the mother of his children. But another part hoped never to see him again. Amy closed her eyes. Then she heard the door of her room open and a thin, middle-aged man in a white coat entered.

"I'm Dr. Riley," he told her. "I'm glad to see you're finally awake! Wish I could say that about all my patients."

He approached the bed and talked to her genially. He told her again of the injuries she had sustained and seemed proud, like the nurse had, that she had come out of the accident with no major ones. He even said she could go home in the morning if she felt up to it.

Amy smiled at this news, never having been one to enjoy hospital visits, let alone hospital stays. But as he talked, she found herself considering if she should ask him if she'd had any other visitors. But wouldn't the nurse have already mentioned it if Devon had come? He probably hadn't come, she told herself. No. He hadn't come.

"Well," the doctor said and he stood to leave. "Is there anything I can get for you? You want some Jell-O or magazines?"

"Do you have a Bible?"

❧ Chapter Fourteen ❧

For the first time, warmth greeted Amy when the fog cleared before her as she opened her eyes to the hilltop before her. But the breeze still blew cool and the leaves moved restlessly at her feet in an unseen tempest.

Gracie waited on the bench. Still waiting. Amy moved closer. Her friend seemed lost in thought and at first didn't notice Amy's approach. Amy hesitated. Gracie looked different somehow... as if she had aged. No longer a young woman of twenty-five, she now more closely resembled a middle-aged woman—even older than Amy. How could this be? But when Gracie's eyes rose to greet her, Amy saw they had not changed.

"I was wondering if I'd get to see you again before..." Gracie broke off and then started over. "I'm glad you're here."

"So am I," Amy said. "I'm glad it finally warmed up a little."

"It has? Hmmm... I hadn't noticed."

Amy joined her on the stone bench, and they sat in silence, absorbing the peace of the place and the comfort of each other's company. Amy noticed the sky no longer appeared quite as gray as it had been on her last visit. Clouds still covered most of the expanse above, but, off to her left, a distinct patch of blue grew ever so slightly.

Fog still surrounded them on all sides, though, and the breeze blew a chill down her back once in a while. Amy tried to adjust her clothing and discovered, to her horror, that she wore only a thin hospital gown with the telltale gap all the way down the back. No wonder she felt a chill!

What am I doing in a hospital gown?

Then it all came back to her. The truck, her broken arm, Idalee's visit, seeing the worry in her children's eyes, the divorce papers—everything.

Gracie noticed Amy's inner struggle and said, "Are you alright, my dear? What's the matter?"

"I'm a little cold in this thing," Amy replied.

"Oh, well, there's your coat."

Amy looked behind her to discover she had been leaning against her warmest winter jacket. She hurriedly put it on and immediately the chill left her.

"Why are you wearing that thin little thing?" Gracie wanted to know. "It looks just like one of those hospital gowns."

"Yes. I believe that's what it is," Amy replied. "You see, I think I'm in the hospital—I mean, I was."

"Don't they even give you back your clothes when you leave anymore?" Gracie was both shocked and disgusted. "That's why I hate hospitals! I avoid them whenever I can."

"Well, I don't think I had much of a choice this time. I was in a car accident and got knocked unconscious. I broke my arm and had a concussion, apparently."

"Your arm looks fine to me."

Amy glanced down and noticed that indeed her arm seemed to be perfectly normal. No cast, and she could move it without the slightest hint of pain. "Oh, well.... I guess it's better here."

"Well, at least you weren't hurt too badly," Gracie smiled. "I'm certainly glad for that!" She gave Amy a quick sideways squeeze. "I think I'd be awfully lonely here if it weren't for your visits."

Amy returned the smile. "You know," she said, wondering how to broach the topic, "while I was in the hospital, I asked the doctor to find me a Bible."

"Oh?" Gracie asked, keenly interested and pleased.

"Yes... I just thought I might try to find out more about some of those things you were telling me earlier. You know, about why God would bother sacrificing Himself for us... whether or not I was one of those people... whether any of it made sense...."

"And? What did you find out?"

"Well, I read all of the book of John... and then I started the book of Luke. I can't claim to have understood all of it. I guess what struck me the most is that reading the Bible is nothing like I thought it'd be."

"What do you mean?"

"I thought it would be either too difficult to understand, too boring, or too outdated to make any real sense in my life. But, when the nurse gave me the sleeping pills and I started to fall asleep, I was actually annoyed I couldn't read more. I didn't want to put it down. I didn't want to stop learning all I could about Jesus." Amy hardly noticed the tears flowing down her cheeks. The bit of sunshine streaming from the growing patch of blue above warmed them on her face. "Nothing I've ever read before has ever affected me this way. Why? How can this be?"

Gracie smiled and her eyes looked suspiciously moist as well. "I suppose it's because every other book is just that—a book. The Bible is God's love letter to His beloved creation—to you, Amy."

"Gracie, I can't say I believe everything I've read... or even that it will always hold this much fascination for me... but I do think maybe, just maybe, there's something more out there—something I've been missing. And I want to find out what it is… or, maybe, Who it is."

☾   ☾   ☾   ☾   ☾

"Well, you're lookin' much better today!" Idalee's voice broke through the quiet of Amy's hospital room the next morning.

"Mom!"

Amy welcomed Cassandra's eager hugs and kisses and then received more from Michael. She ignored the ache in her arm and neck in favor of her children's affection. They both seemed genuinely relieved to be back with her again, despite the surroundings.

"So, the doc says you're going home this morning," Idalee said brightly. "That's good! You sure gave us a scare, Amy! Don't think I'm going to forgive you for that any time soon!"

Amy gave her an appreciative glance. "Just help me get my stuff together, would you?"

Idalee started scouring the room for Amy's few belongings. She packed up Amy's backpack with not only Amy's things, but several hospital items as well, including the plastic pitcher, a water bottle with the hospital logo on it, and a stack of extra bandages. Amy ignored her friend's questionable packing style in favor of hearing how her children had fared without her last night.

"We had fun," Michael said. "Idalee let us stay up late and watch a movie and eat popcorn."

"So late? And, on a school night?" Amy asked with mock annoyance.

"Well, it's not like we had to go this morning," Michael answered. "We had to come help you get home from the hospital."

"And we got to play Monopoly, too," Cassandra resumed, her eyes large with excitement, "and I won!"

"Well," Michael rephrased, "part of the evening was fun, anyway."

"But we missed you an awful lot," Cassandra said, with an immediate change of expression.

"Sounds like it," Amy replied with good-humored sarcasm. "If I'd have been there you'd have been in bed on time."

"Now, now," Idalee said from across the room, rear-end in the air. Her words came out in a strange gasp as she bent over to look under the small dresser. "They were too worried to sleep! They needed the diversion. I can take them to school as soon as we get you home."

"What did you watch?" Amy asked her children.

"We watched Jurassic Park II!" Cassandra said with large, frightened eyes.

"Well, that's a diversion, alright!" Amy replied. "I guess it's hard to worry about your mother's broken arm when people are getting eaten by dinosaurs."

☾   ☾   ☾   ☾   ☾

Something banged. Monica opened her eyes onto a sight that was at first confusing. A woman in a over-sized, pale blue shirt bustled about clumsily in her room.

Monica blinked. Why did her neck ache so? But, no. This wasn't her room. It was a hospital room—her mother's hospital room—and today was Wednesday.

Monica glanced at the round, black-ringed clock on the wall. Still too early to bother the others. The nurse made an apologetic expression for waking her, and Monica smiled a pardon in return. She yawned, rubbed her neck, and looked at her mother. Nothing had changed. Sleep still reigned.

The nurse finally left. Monica rose from the large, under-stuffed chair that had been her bed and stepped into the miniscule bathroom to wash her face and run a comb through her hair. Soon Daniel would be here, bringing Celia or Kevin or someone to relieve her watch. But Monica was content to stay a bit longer... with her mother.

As she again took her place on the stiff chair, a bland exhaustion settled on Monica. She remembered now all the many times throughout the night that nurses had disturbed her sleep. She remembered the many times she had battled discomfort, searching for a way to rest her head without it falling over at a weird angle against her shoulder. But none of that really mattered. She looked at her mother.

"Mom," she said aloud, as if she were simply trying to wake her from a light slumber. She remembered what Dr. Riley had said. Her mother could not survive another heart attack. "Mom, wake up." Silence. Monica sighed. "Mom. Wake up, please."

A rattling noise came from the hall. Monica watched an orderly push a cart with one loose wheel past the partially open door to her mother's room. All the implements on the cart jiggled noisily. Steel on steel. Monica listened as the sound lessened and then stopped, presumably outside the door of a room down the hall.

Monica rose from the chair and took a seat in a straight-backed chair next to the bed, near her mother's head.

"Mom. Please. Wake up."

Silence... except for the distant laughter of the nurses at the nurses' station down the hall. Monica turned her back to the noise.

"Mom. It's Monica. Can't you wake up? Please?"

Nothing.

Monica rubbed her forehead and dragged her hand roughly across her cheek, staving off emotion.

"Can't you hear me? Mom? Please. Just wake up. How hard could that be? Please. Do it for me." Monica paused. Reason fought with feelings of rejection.

"You would wake up if you could," she finally admitted. "I know you would. Maybe you're trying... but just can't."

Monica sighed. A single tear ran down her left cheek. She wiped it away with barely a thought. Tears had become such a natural part of living. She looked at her mother—the sunken eyes, the fragile, ill-looking skin. Hair unkempt from lack of washing and combing. Could this really be the same woman? The difference was remarkable. Monica remembered the last time she had seen her mother on her last visit three years ago. Monica and Manuél had brought their children for Thanksgiving and stayed three weeks. Her mother had been vibrant, energetic... alive. Now. Now she was something else.

"Mom!" Monica nearly yelled. "Wake up!"

A sob broke the last words and she buried her face in her hands.

"I'm sorry, Mom. I'm s-sorry."

She sniffed and wiped her eyes, trying to gather herself.

"I don't want to yell at you. I just want you to hear me. Can you hear me? I wish you could! ...There's so much I could tell you about our lives in Mexico. Did you know Angel is thinking of going to school in the States? And Charity—Charity is such a young lady! You would barely recognize her! She's so much like her father... full of natural charm and...." Monica trailed off. She swallowed back fresh tears.

"Are you leaving us, Mom? Are you going to leave us?"

Monica sat in silence waiting for the response she knew would not come. Heavy breaths escaped her lips.

Dear Lord, help me, please.

She closed her eyes and took another long, deep breath. Opening them again, she saw her mother. She saw the mother who had been strong when others would have crumbled. She saw the mother who trusted God when others would have flung curses at Him. She saw the mother who had so often spoken about how wonderful life in Heaven would be.

"It's okay, Mom," she said in a surprisingly calm voice, despite of the tears now running freely down her cheeks. She took her mother's hand in hers. "It's okay. You can go home if you want to. God will take care of us for you. He'll take care of us. He'll take care of me."

Monica heard a shuffling behind her. She turned around to see Angel hovering uncertainly at the door. She smiled and reached a hand toward him. His look was one of relief mixed with concern as he approached her quickly and took her hand. She stood and pulled him into a warm embrace. She had to reach up now, he was so big.

"Are you alright, Mom?" he asked with an almost imperceptible Spanish accent.

"I will be. I will be."

❧ Chapter Fifteen ❧

Upon her return from the hospital, Amy discovered several new aches and bruises. Everything hurt. Even the prescribed painkillers didn't take the pain away completely. That Thursday afternoon, she slowly and clumsily climbed onto her bed to take a nap, knowing Idalee promised to pick the kids up from school and take them to her house for the afternoon so Amy could get some extra rest. Amy was grateful. But even though she'd had the entire morning to rest, she hadn't.

At first, she struggled to get her mind off that envelope of divorce papers still hidden on top of the refrigerator. She hadn't looked at them since returning home yesterday; nor had she shown them to anyone. The children didn't know yet. Neither did Idalee. Amy hid the terrible secret in her own heart and mind for now. But her Bible had been open a lot this last day and a half.

Amy sighed and closed her eyes. So many things to worry about... the divorce, her banged up car, her battered body, the hospital bills... and yet, for some reason, none of it really seemed to matter. Something else grew to the forefront of her mind, something more important, something good.

"Hello, there," Gracie greeted her with a smile. She still looked aged, but her smile and eyes filled with genuine pleasure at the sight of Amy approaching across the grass. Most of the leaves had been blown away and, despite the fog still hovering at the borders of the hilltop, the air around their stone bench looked brighter and clearer. "I see you're dressed more appropriately this time."

Amy smiled, glad to be finally rid of the hospital getup and back in jeans.

"Yes!" she agreed and took her place next to her friend.

A warm line of sunshine beamed on Amy's face, but, somehow, shadows still surrounded Gracie. Her brow still furrowed with anxiety.

"How are you today?" Amy asked.

"I feel... strange...." Gracie answered, uncertain. "I seem to be getting... farther away."

"What do you mean?"

"Oh, I don't know," Gracie turned and waved her hand as if to dismiss the subject. "Never mind. I shouldn't worry about such piddly matters. How are you doing?"

"I think... I think I'm actually doing okay. Don't ask me to explain it! I've never had a worse week in my entire life! But... somehow I think everything is going to be okay."

Gracie smiled.

"My husband, Devon... he sent me divorce papers," Amy continued. "And I don't know what to do about it."

"Who says you're supposed to do anything?"

"You mean, I shouldn't sign them? Even after all he's done?"

"If your husband really wants a divorce, he'll find a way to get one, whether you sign those papers or not. Why make it easy for him? Besides, who knows what may happen down the road. Let God handle that. Let God handle Devon. You have more important things to concern yourself with, anyway."

"Things more important than my impending divorce?" Amy said, her skepticism showing in her tone.

"Absolutely," Gracie responded without a shred of doubt. "You have your children... and you have a new love. Am I right?"

Amy smiled. She thought of all the miraculous things she'd discovered in John and Luke.

"I suppose I do."

"I think right now your main concern should be with Him. Spend time with Him. Read His love letter to you. Talk with Him. Then, when that relationship is a healthy one, you will know how to face your other relationships in a healthy way, too."

"I'm so glad I've met you, Gracie. It's as if I've met an angel."

For an instant Amy wondered if somehow she really had.

But Gracie laughed. "Oh, I'm far from being an angel, I'm afraid."

Amy smiled back. For a few moments, they sat together silently absorbing the thin sunshine. It felt warm on Amy's face.

Gracie sighed, not an altogether peaceful sound. Amy turned to look at her. "Something on your mind?"

"Nothing new. I just still wish I could leave this place—go home. My family needs me. There's so much to do."

"I seem to recall something you said earlier. Let's see... didn't you say, 'What makes us think that we can do everything on our own? What makes us think that we were even meant to?' Wasn't that it?"

Gracie turned to her friend with a look of wonder on her face.

"I suppose I did," she said slowly. "You're right."

Amy smiled. "Maybe if God can take care of me, He can take care of your family, too."

Gracie's face contorted as a sob escaped her lips.

"Oh, I'm sorry!" Amy was immediately flustered. "I didn't mean to...."

"No. It's okay, sweetie. You're right," Gracie said through tears. She took a deep breath, and as her lungs filled with fresh air, her body filled with color. Pink skin, blue eyes, and the white hair of a much older woman.

How beautiful, Amy thought in wonder, gazing at her friend. But Gracie didn't notice Amy's surprise.

Gracie continued, "I think maybe God's been doing just that—all along. And He knew I just needed to see it through someone else's eyes—through the eyes of a friend."

Amy glanced away smiling, embarrassed by the compliment. It felt both strange and wondrous to know that God—who she was really just getting to know—would choose to use her to help someone else—even if it was just a dream person. For, truly, Gracie had become so much more to Amy.

"Oh, look," Amy heard Gracie say in a voice full of wonder. "Spring has come."

With the spring, vibrant color permeated their hilltop, dominating the shifting black and white waves and overtaking everything before her. As she watched, bits of brilliant color began to sprout through the browns and dull greens, as hundreds of tiny flowers bloomed before their eyes. The flowers dotted the hilltop and delicate tendrils of climbing vines crawled up the legs of the bench. New leaves popped out in bright green brilliance on the branches of the few trees. The fog grew thinner and thinner as the sunlight grew stronger and warmer, chasing away the dark and the chill and the fear. A sweet scent filled the air—a fragrance like none other—strong and sweet, creating a pleasant, peaceful sensation within her chest—like hope.

Then, Amy felt a soft, warm wind blow through her hair from where her friend was seated. But when Amy turned to look, she realized she was alone. Gracie had vanished.

☾   ☾   ☾   ☾   ☾

Daniel and Celia had just arrived at the hospital to relieve Louisa when Mother Bennett's heart monitor made that same terrifying beep. Immediately, the room swarmed with nurses and doctors and they were again ushered from the room to the waiting room. They waited for less than a half hour before Dr. Riley came in with a sad expression on his face. They knew. She hadn't survived. Mother Bennett had passed away.

Soon the rest of the family gathered at Mother Bennett's home. They sat together in her large living room. Some cried silently. Others just stood looking nowhere in particular. Others sat in silence. Louisa busied herself in the kitchen making sandwiches.

"Well, she's with Jesus now... and Dad," Daniel said.

"You know..." Monica said with a look of wonder peering through glistening eyes, "I never thought I'd say this, but I'm glad... I mean, think of how wonderful everything must be for her now. I think, maybe, we should be happy for her. She's finally receiving her reward."

"I suppose it would be selfish of us to want her back now," Celia agreed.

"And it's not like we won't see her again," Angel said.

"But we'll sure miss her in the meantime," Louisa said, having listened from the kitchen doorway. "There are things I think I'd like to discuss with her... from time to time."

"I suppose we'll just have to discuss those things with each other," Kevin said. He crossed the room and put an arm around his wife's shoulders and gave her an affectionate squeeze. "And with God."

"Jes," Manuél joined. "He weel never leave us. Of dat we can be sure."

☾   ☾   ☾   ☾   ☾

Amy drove along Highway 8 on her way home from a job interview for a secretarial position, feeling pleased at how it had gone. She had heard of the job opening from her friend Anne at church and had decided to give it a shot.

She drove her 'new' used car that insurance had mostly covered. The accident, now three weeks behind her, left her eager to move on with her life and make changes for the better. The divorce papers remained unsigned, despite several angry phone messages and texts she'd received from both Devon and Darla. If she were completely honest with herself, frustrating their plans brought her a secret pleasure. But Amy's determination stemmed primarily from the desire to trust God in the meantime and, ultimately, do the right thing—even if that meant not doing anything at all.

As Amy turned left at the street that would take her home, she happened to glance up at the hilltop cemetery she had often passed. As she drove by, the sight of a small stone bench caught her eye. It looked exactly like the one in her dreams. Tempted to slam on the brakes, memories of her recent accident lent her better instincts, so she slowed and drove safely onto the shoulder. Once parked inside the cemetery gates, she nearly ran over to the stone bench.

It's the same! It's the exact same bench!

"So strange...." she mumbled as she ran her hand along the identical seat and backing, her fingers remembering the feel of it.

She turned and sat down. Looking around, she noticed that even the lay of the terrain resembled her dream hilltop—except for the many headstones dotting this hill.

"Amazing.... I've never been here… but I have."

Amy sat there for a few moments absorbing her awe and enjoying the sunshine. She glanced across the hill to where it flattened out just a small jaunt below. Many headstone populated that area, but a pair of people standing near a freshly filled grave caught her attention. A petite, brunette woman stood with a young man at her side. He appeared to be a teenager.

Amy assumed they were mother and son. She watched as the woman dabbed her eyes with a handkerchief. Then she saw a sight that warmed her heart. The young man put an arm around his mother and hugged her. The woman smiled at her son and then they turned and headed toward a waiting vehicle.

Amy followed their car with her eyes until it was out of sight. After they left, Amy decided to take a short stroll through the cemetery before returning home. Her children wouldn't be home for another hour yet.

Soon her feet took her close to where the woman and her son had been standing. Amy's curiosity got the better of her, so she stepped nearer and read the inscription on the tombstone. She gasped in utter amazement! It read:

GRACIE BENNETT, BELOVED MOTHER AND
GRANDMOTHER, MAY SHE FIND REST IN THE
HANDS OF JESUS. ROMANS 15:13.

"Gracie! Could it be? Beloved mother...." Amy said slowly. "Amy," she said her own name aloud, liking the sound of it. "Beloved.... And there's that verse! Romans 15:13.... May the God of hope fill you with all joy and peace as you trust in Him, so that you may overflow with hope by the power of the Holy Spirit," she quoted aloud from memory. She sighed, not really understanding and yet knowing something miraculous had taken place in her life.

Amy's mind went to her wedding day. She had been so happy! So expectant! She had believed her marriage to Devon would last a lifetime. But it hadn't... and now she faced a myriad of questions and sorrows. She could see a long road in front of her... and yet something new grew in her heart—something that made the road less daunting, less dark.

Her mind returned to the promises she had read in her Bible—the promises John had written about—how by believing in Jesus, she could claim the right to be called a child of God. She smiled and her eyes misted momentarily. But these were no longer tears of sorrow drowned in exhaustion. Now Amy knew hope—true hope. And now she could rest in the hope that comes only from Jesus Christ.

She marveled. How could this be? How could this mystery be taking place? In the midst of agonizing heartbreak, she had somehow fallen deeply, desperately, passionately in love with Jesus! And she knew this love would last far beyond a mere lifetime.

THE END

More From
The Dramatic Pen

@TDPPress
www.TheDramaticPen.com
Facebook.com/TheDramaticPen

The Scrolls of the Nevi'im Series:

Book I: Habakkuk's Plea: A Prophet of Elohim
Book II: Habakkuk's Plea: Evil Persists
Book III: Habakkuk's Plea: Elohim Answers
By S. E. Thomas, M.A.

The Sixth Hour
Book I of the Holy Land Mysteries
Series
By S. E. Thomas

Can Darash, a Jewish teenager, track a killer, rescue his family from ruin, and discover the truth about Yeshua? The rebel, Yeshua, drove the merchants and moneychangers from the Temple with a whip. Hours later, one of them was murdered. Now fifteen-year-old Darash must find a way to protect his family from poverty even as he struggles with the grief of losing his father. When another murder is committed, Darash finds himself searching for a dangerous killer and relying on an old, blind basket-weaver for help. Despite the odds, Darash discovers he has strength of character, a deep compassion for others, and an uncanny knack for problem-solving. But will he be able to expose the killer before the killer finds him?

The Holy Land Mysteries Series

Darash's adventures continue with…
Book II: The Brazen Altar
Book III: The Mud Flower
Book IV: The Leper's Gift
Book V: The Weeping Place
And More!

Into the Beautiful
Poetry by Montana Artists
Series

"Into the Beautiful: Poetry by Montana Artists" is a series of poetry books by Montana artists of all ages. These works of art and creativity were collected through annual contests run August through October 15th. To find out more about this contest, please visit our website at www.TheDramaticPen.com.

Who Invited The Stiff to Dinner?
An Interactive Mystery Party Game
for Teens and Adults

The guests arrive for a distinguished dinner party at the wealthy English estate of Richard Orwell Mortice. But why would he invite so many of his enemies into his home, along with a Scotland Yard Inspector? When the maid discovers good ol' Rick O. Mortice dead, the Inspector and his overly eager Lieutenant sidekick are out to discover the culprit! Everyone has a motive, and the accusations fly—but not before they go ahead and sit down to a luxurious meal. After all, why let one stiff ruin dinner? *(Requires 15 participants. Includes full, reproducible script, invitation templates, nametags, place settings, and a full set of host/hostess directions. Templates available online for free download.)*

S. E. Thomas
Artwork by Yesenia A. Thomas

Murder at Surly Gates
An Interactive Mystery Party Game
for Teens and Adults

Tensions are high when the cantankerous residents of Surly Gates Nursing Home have to put up with money-hungry relatives, a spoiled brat, and her incompetent mother during visitors' hours. When the nursing home manager turns up dead in his office, everyone is a suspect! Who had something to gain from his death? What happened to Badger's heart pills? Why does Lily, a former beauty queen, still try to swing her hips—even behind her walker? Buster, a resident and former security guard, and his son, Doyle, a bumbling cop, want to solve this case! *(Requires 15 participants. Includes full, reproducible script, invitation templates, nametags, place settings, and a full set of host/hostess directions. Templates available online for free download.)*

S. E. Thomas
Artwork by Yesenia A. Thomas

Accuracy
An Interactive Mystery Party Game
for Teens or Adults

A successful, but pompous, author is murdered on the night of his new book debut celebration. A note—intended to stop the murder—actually spurns the killer into action due to some rearranged punctuation. Who wrote the note? Who tampered with the note? Who carried out the false instructions? Nearly everyone has a motive! An intelligent Spanish lawyer with a very thick accent discovers the truth. *(Requires 11 participants. Includes full, reproducible script, invitation templates, nametags, place settings, and a full set of host/hostess directions. Templates available online for free download.)*

Let Them Eat Cake
An Interactive Mystery Party Game
for Teens or Adults
By S. E. Thomas

A reputable cake-baking contest is underway and the contestants are vying to win 20% of the stock in the wealthy contest sponsor's restaurant business. Then the sponsor turns up dead! He ate an entire cake ridden with arsenic-bearing apple seeds! Who gave him the cake? Who wanted him dead? Why in the world didn't he stop at the first bite? A bumbling security guard who is allergic to flour is on the case! *(Requires 14 participants.)*

A Reason To Celebrate
A Full-Length Christmas
Production

For most, Christmas is a time filled with joy. But for many, Christmas can be a difficult season. Some of us may even feel that Christmas is not a time of celebration, but of sorrow…. But let us consider a moment what Scripture tells us of the first Christmas. What really happened? For the first time, God Himself—the Creator of the Universe, the King of Kings, the Everlasting Father—stepped into our world! He stepped in—not to enjoy the wealth or the beauty or the joys—but to experience our suffering, our longings, and our sorrows. And, even from the moment of His birth, He experienced far from ideal circumstances. And yet, we remember His words, "In this world you will have trouble. But take heart! I have overcome the world."

Sourdough Secrets… Revealed!
From Making the Starter to
Sourdough Success!
By Ray Templeton

Step-by-step instructions that will allow you to make your own starter, make your first loaf, and even learn to make sourdough bread in your bread machine.

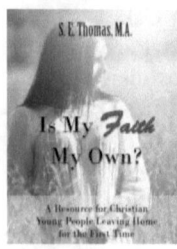

Is My Faith My Own?
A Resource for Christian Young People
Leaving Home for the First Time
By S. E. Thomas

Everything was going along fine... then you got out on your own and realized it's your responsibility to get the rest of your life right. From here on out, if you're going to follow God, you're going to be doing it on your own. You can no longer coast by on your parents' faith, your pastor's understanding, or your youth leader's morals. Now it's up to you. And you have some questions: Is my faith real? Is it growing? Is it my own? (A *Finding Hope Resource Guide*.)

Does God See Me?
Finding Hope in the Midst
of an Unplanned Pregnancy
By S.E. Thomas

When Hagar was a little girl she dreamed of being a wife and mother. She never dreamed of being pregnant, alone, and destitute. But life has a way of surprising us. Suddenly she found her head and heart swimming with fears—fears voiced as questions: Why did this happen to me? What am I going to do? Who will love me now? But most of all, Hagar needed to know: Does God see me? (A *Finding Hope Resource Guide*.)

Please Visit Us Again!

Find books, study guides, plays, skits, mystery party games, fundraising resources, free downloadable program templates, writers' resources, and more:

www.TheDramaticPen.com
Write To Bless The World

www.ingramcontent.com/pod-product-compliance
Lightning Source LLC
Chambersburg PA
CBHW050952120626
46552CB00001B/502